IAN R MITCHELL taught history in further education for over twenty years, specialising in German history. During that time he wrote a standard textbook on Germany under Bismarck and visited the former GDR (East Germany) several times. On leaving teaching Ian made his reputation as a mountaineering writer with such titles (co-authored with Dave Brown) as *Mountain Days and Bothy Nights* and *A View from the Ridge*. The latter won the Boardman-Tasker Prize for Mountain Literature in 1991. In 1998 his *Scotland's Mountains before the Mountaineers* won the Outdoor Writers' Guild Award for Excellence. Ian has also had several of his short stories published in literary magazines and a collection of his mountaineering fiction, *The Mountain Weeps*, was published in 1997. His acclaimed historical novel, *Mountain Outlaw*, appeared in 2003.

By the same author:

Bismarck, Holmes McDougall, 1980

Mountain Days and Bothy Nights (with Dave Brown), Luath Press, 1987

The First Munroist (with Pete Drummond), The Ernest Press, 1993

Second Man on the Rope, Mercat Press, 1995

Mountain Footfalls, Mercat Press, 1996

The Mountain Weeps, Stobcross Press, 1997

Scotland's Mountains before the Mountaineers, Luath Press, 1998

On the Trail of Queen Victoria in the Highlands, Luath Press, 2000

Mountain Outlaw, Luath Press, 2003

This City Now: Glasgow and its working class past, Luath Press, 2005

Walking through Scotland's History, Luath Press, 2007

A View from the Ridge (with Dave Brown), Luath Press, 2007

Winter in Berlin

or

The Mitropa Smile

Ian R Mitchell

Luath Press Limited

EDINBURGH

www.luath.co.uk

First published 2009

ISBN: 978-1-906817-10-7

The paper used in this book is recyclable. It is made from low
chlorine pulps produced in a low energy, low emissions manner
from renewable forests.

The publisher acknowledges subsidy from

Scottish
Arts Council

towards the publication of this volume

Printed and bound by Bell & Bain Ltd., Glasgow

Typeset in 11 point Sabon

Author's Preface

AT A POINT late on in *Winter in Berlin* mention is made of Sir Walter Scott, the inventor of the historical novel. The initial fate of his first effort in the genre, *Waverley*, mirrors in some ways that of the present work. Thinking that at the height of the Napoleonic wars no one would be interested in a tale of the Jacobite conflict, Scott left the manuscript unattended for ten or so years before offering it for publication.

I originally wrote *Winter in Berlin* over the period 1986 to 1988. Soon afterwards the GDR disappeared and thereafter a few enquiries made me realise that no one was interested in publishing fiction about the departed state. Works about the *Wende*, the collapse of the GDR, were then all the rage. Twenty years later I feel that the content of the book may now be of more interest, though the reader is entitled to ask what I have changed. The answer is, relatively little. Like a lamp or a pair of old shoes long unused in a cupboard, I have given little more than a polish.

I have added some details to improve the authenticity of the portrayal of *alltagsleben* in the former state, but this is not a rewritten work intending to be pregnant with foresight as to the end of the GDR. Any hints to the contrary a reader might pick up are unintended and have not been added subsequently. When I wrote *Winter in Berlin* I assumed – as did the supporters of the state, its opponents and the indifferent – that the GDR might, like Prussia, not last forever, but in no way did I foresee its imminent or even medium-term collapse. This is important, since the characters make their choices on the assumption of the stability of the GDR.

Winter in Berlin is set in the GDR in the early 1980s at a time of heightening Cold War tensions, the imposition of martial law in neighbouring Poland and the Soviet intervention in Afghanistan. In the tradition of the German *Novelle*, the work is a long short story, or short novel. It is limited in time and place to the elucidation and development of key ideas and characters, but mainly to that of the central character who comes to realise the limited nature of the impact it is possible to make on historical and political events.

Winter in Berlin expresses, I hope, authenticity of setting and familiarity with the complexity of 'the German Problem' and its GDR expression. Its publication marks the twentieth anniversary of the fall of the Berlin Wall and the collapse of the old GDR, an apposite time.

'Winter kept us warm' (TS Eliot, *The Waste Land*)

'Man makes history, but not under conditions of his own choosing' (Karl Marx)

Rioting in Gdansk

Serious rioting broke out yesterday in Gdansk, as Poles awoke to find that prices of basic foods had doubled, trebled and in some cases quadrupled overnight. Police battled with workers at the Lenin shipyard and over 200 people were arrested. The city has been sealed off and a curfew imposed.

These are the most serious disturbances to have occurred in Poland since martial law was imposed by the government of General Jaruzelski a month ago, and the establishment then of a Military Council of National Salvation to run the country. This crackdown on the Solidarity trades union movement led to the arrest of 14,000 people and the deaths of seven miners in Silesia in confrontations with troops.

CHAPTER ONE

'*Es ist noch Winter in Berlin.*'

The voice drew the scholar's eyes away from watching the tide of people, swaddled against the intense cold, moving around him part hidden by their condensing breaths. The middle-aged woman, rotund in her enveloping coat, smiled at him. She was clutching to her a token of visible recognition – the historical publication with which he was to become familiar in the weeks ahead. They stood awkwardly on the concourse steps of the Friedrichstrasse station. Behind them sat the diners in the Mitropa restaurant, around them moved the silent throng of home-going Berliners.

He replied with a stumbled sentence of agreement about the cold, in the German which he had not used for some years. Then the woman hustled him out of the concourse and onto the street, through the station arch where the *Ausgang* sign glowed dully. Here was a taxi rank, with a patiently waiting queue, muffled against the chill. Opposite, another neon sign combatted the darkness and advertised the *Theater Metropol*. Taxis slowly reduced the line of waiting figures who occasionally stamped feet and clapped arms against the cold. Yes, it was winter still.

His companion talked, with intermissions where he nodded agreement or indicated his comprehension. But his attention was distracted by the street, the people, the buildings around. His eye caught a metal plaque beside the station *Eingang* sign, just behind where he stood. In the dark he could initially make out only isolated words; then '*hingerichtet*' jolted him and he strained to read further. Here the ss had hung two youths for refusing to fight the Red Army in the Battle of Berlin. But before he could read all of the inscription, he realised that he was being pushed into a taxi – a Lada saloon – and the driver, nodding, was being given instructions, repeated to avoid error. The woman then paid the driver: from the back seat he noted it was a 12-mark fare. He knew travel was cheap here, so that signified a long journey.

Through the open front window she spoke to him, seated in the back, reminding him, '*Bis Morgen. Acht Uhr. Punkt.*'

The taxi moved through broad deserted boulevards, across the silent sleeping city. Shop fronts were shuttered and house windows blinded. Occasionally the low street lights revealed a pedestrian, or illuminated the branches of trees on the pavements, totally bare of leaves. At major road junctions were small illuminated grey kiosks, inside which sat the *Vopos*, the People's Police. The heavily frosted streets gave back the chill lamp light. Ten, fifteen minutes passed; they seemed to have a distance to cover. The driver was silent and his passenger fell into a reverie. *Noch Winter...*

He had journeyed by train. He preferred the train because it did not bring about the sudden crude juxtapositions of distance-annihilating flight. The train allowed you to adjust to the change of scene, absorb the variation of social context. On this journey especially, he felt the need for that adjustment. His method of transport had caused the Cultural Mission enormous problems, especially when he specified his desired route as via Hamburg (to visit the Bismarck *Denkmal*). A phone call from London had coupled him with an urbane and amused representative of the Foreign Tours Department.

'I'm afraid you'll have to come via London. The Hamburg route hasn't operated since the war.'

Another provincial was thus put in his place. And via London he had gone.

At home, incipient spring had been in evidence. Late January was mild and in London the trees showed buds. But after he boarded the Mitropa train from the night boat across the channel and began to travel east, it became colder. As the miles of the German plain were crossed, the train was heading towards midwinter. Though the journey was one of monotonous flatness – forest and field, field and forest, forest and field – it was akin to an ascent of a winter's mountain. At first a light frost, then snow patches, finally solid ice. By the time the Elbe was crossed, the ground was fast with snow in all directions and the river moved under grinding floes of ice.

'There's so much snow, it's been setting off the mines

at the Wall with the weight.'

This contribution to the silent coach came from a cheerful and restless young man, but failed to bring more than a nod and a weak smile in turn from the two other passengers. The youth exited at Hannover, leaving the compartment to the travelling scholar and an elderly woman, knitting. After a while, the silence was broken by the woman.

'*Sie gehen nach Berlin?*'

The scholar concurred. The silence was resumed as he gazed out at the snow-spread fields and the trees, their branches pulled down by the snow. She pursued her enquiries and asked if he was with 'the occupying powers'. His foreignness must have been evident from his accent. He smiled.

'*Nein, ich gehe nach Ost Berlin. Um zu studieren.*'

She looked surprised, picked up her knitting and then laid it down again. He added that he was British and was going to study at the Humboldt University.

She seemed to want to say something, but instead lifted up her needles and worked them swiftly. Then, in English,

'People in West Germany say nothing good about the DDR.'

She continued to knit very rapidly until they were told by the guard who came to check their tickets that they would soon be approaching the frontier. She searched her handbag and pulled out a passport. It was a West German one. She noticed him looking.

'I came from the East, Osten. *Flüchtling*, refugee. My husband, my children stayed there. In Chemnitz.' She smiled, then corrected herself, 'Karl Marx Stadt. I can go and see them now, it is easier. Before, they would not let me go back to visit. Things are getting easier in the DDR.'

Silence fell again as the train slowed down, nearing the border zone. His seat faced east, so he could see down the line. Ahead of the train a set of watchtowers confirmed the proximity of the frontier. The train crawled forwards and entered a deep forest separated from the track on each side by a high boundary fence. The forest's symmetry betrayed it as a plantation. The train inched on past the guard towers and the woman knitted, paying no attention. Familiar with all this. Fire breaks split the forest and in these were tethered dogs, which barked at the train. He could not hear them but could see their cold breath of anger. On the path that ran inside the fence there were occasional military vehicles occupied by young soldiers.

After possibly half a mile of slow progress the train stopped at a platform occupied only by soldiers and border officials. It might have once served a former village razed to create the border zone. The train, almost empty, stood silent. Nothing happened, or appeared to happen, for a long time. He opened the window and saw that the border guards were running mirrors underneath the train. In the background the dogs still barked, and now he could hear them. A tap on the shoulder turned him round. A uniformed member of the *Grenzpolizei*, with an absurdly youthful face, like one of his students at home, stood in the carriage.

'*Reisepass*,' demanded the frontier guard, and stood motionless.

He handed over his passport. The guard stared at the visa, with its hammer and compass logo, giving the bearer the right to stay in Berlin for three months. The photograph was carefully studied. Its owner volunteered the information that he used to wear his hair longer. The guard ignored this and instead pointed to the US visa.

'*Sie waren in Amerika?*'

He concurred and in reply to the question of how he had found it there, replied, '*Interessant.*'

The guard smiled and handed back the passport.

'*Gute Reise.*'

Waving aside the old lady's proffered passport, he moved off down the almost empty train.

Interessant. Yes, it had been interesting, those thousands of miles of nothing, of desert and wheat fields, between San Francisco and Boston. The opulence of Amarillo and Albuquerque, the clapboard slums in the middle of nowhere of the Mexicans and Negroes. The kind and gentle fellow passengers on the Greyhound bus who asked you to visit them, and meant it, but who you knew had forgotten you the instant they descended, taking with them their fantasies. The life stories they told you on first meeting, full of court-room and hospital drama. And their desire to bomb somebody far away: Iran, Libya, Cuba, it did not seem to matter. He had listened, fascinated, to these well-mannered, perpetual adolescents, understanding why a second-rate movie ham had just become elected as the arbiter of the world's destiny.

That had been interesting: but so was this, he thought, looking at the line which divided the world surer than any meridian. *Auch interessant* slipped unbidden into his mind. He was slowly adjusting.

After standing for about half an hour, the train started again. The German plain was little different this side of the frontier, the same landscape of forest and field, field and forest, as the train moved relentlessly east. The rivers they now crossed were solid with ice. 'The very dead of winter', he quoted to himself. How did the lines go after that, he tried to recall. Something about the journey being all folly.

He noticed little traffic on the country roads, many of which were cobbled, like the streets in the town on the edge of the cold Germanic Ocean where he had been born.

He moved down the train to the Mitropa buffet, where there were no other customers. The waiter served him, breaking off a card game with the cook. The scholar had eaten nothing since London and the food was more than welcome. As he drank his coffee darkness fell and there was nothing more to see outside, except blackness and his own reflection staring back at him from the window. His mind ran over the impressions of the day, then pushed them aside, clearing the way for the thought that was drummed into his head by the rhythm of the train's wheels: 'What am I doing this for? What am I doing this for?' The wheels repeated the question endlessly without answering it. Was it 'all folly'?

Again the train began to slow down. The cook and waiter had returned to their card game. The carriage shuddered as the train stopped. Going to the window again, he looked down the line. Dazzling light filled the distance, so bright it initially blinded him. As his eyes blinked and refocused, he sensed, rather than discerned what lay ahead.

'*Die Mauer*,' confirmed the cook, without interrupting the game.

Now the train was flanked by concrete walls as it moved forwards. A little beyond the glare it stopped at a small station crowded with people. Some of them got on. Where was he? Confused, he turned to the Mitropa crew. They were used to this. Before he could ask anything, the waiter gave an answer.

'*Bleiben sie ruhig. Sie sind in West Berlin.*'

On restarting, the train passed over streets ablaze with light and frantic with cars. Then it stopped for a second time and most if not all of the other passengers got off. Berlin Zoo, he read, and again looked to the card players for advice.

'*Immer noch West Berlin.*'

This time it was the cook who spoke, following with a smile as he trumped his opponent.

The train waited, the scholar watched. Later he would know the solution to the problem that confused him; the railways in West Berlin were still run by the East German *Reichsbahn*, the last link between the two sections of the city. Now it was a disorienting but mildly pleasant confusion. The train slowly moved over a river he assumed was the Spree. Once more the blaze of light, followed by darkness. Then, eyes adjusting slowly to dimmer light, he looked along a deserted platform.

Berlin Friedrichstrasse. Berlin Friedrichstrasse. Berlin Friedrichstrasse. Berlin Friedrichstrasse. Deserted, except for a couple of policemen.

As the train stopped, the cook announced with the ironic smile he would grow used to, that Mitropa smile, '*Berlin, Hauptstadt der* DDR. *Wilkommen!*'

Going back to the carriage to collect his luggage, he noticed that the old lady had gone, had probably descended at the zoo station. He got off alone and scanned the platform for the *Ausgang* sign, located one. Descending a flight of stairs below it, he passed a small kiosk where a woman, knitting furiously like some Norn, offered tax-free spirits and cigarettes. In the foyer below, against the far wall, were other kiosks – passport control. He chose the central one and handed over his document. The guard flicked through it, looked him up and down. Then he was given a list of prohibited imports. Did he have any of these? Though he knew the list, he glanced at it for form's sake. Military toys, drugs, pornography, anti-socialist literature.

'*Nein.*'

A buzz. A light flashed red, the metal door like a football turnstile swung round, and he was facing another door. Once through it, he found himself in the concourse of Friedrichstrasse station. Tiled in yellow and black and with the cut glass and neon lettering of the shops and restaurant, it recalled Western décor of twenty years ago, when he was a young man. Briefly, he felt as if he had moved back across all these years.

The concourse was crowded with people queuing for tickets or heading for the domestic train services that also used Friedrichstrasse station. He had been told he would be met, but had not been given any details.

'Look for someone looking for someone,' he thought.

At the back of the hall, on the vantage point of the steps, he saw a head bobbing, eyes darting. Below was held – deliberately – a copy of a magazine. That was his contact. He walked towards the bearer, noting the confirmation on the magazine cover: *Zeitschrift für Geschichtswissenschaft*. She clutched his arm with her free hand and greeted him warmly. As if she knew me, he thought.

'*Komm*,' she said. Then, stepping back, she eyed his warm winter coat with approval.

'*Gut, gut bekleidet. Es is noch Winter in Berlin.*'

Brezhnev Denounces US Arms to Mujihadeen

Several hundred Soviet and Afghan soldiers have been burned alive or suffocated in a fire inside the Salang Pass tunnel. The fire began after two vehicles collided in the one and a half mile long tunnel. Soviet troops mistook the resulting explosion for a rebel attack and closed the tunnel, trapping traffic inside. Later Soviet leader Leonid Brezhnev paid tribute to the soldiers who died and said the incident would not weaken the determination of the Red Army to defend The People's Afghanistan against its bandit opponents aided by international imperialism, and he specifically denounced the flow of American arms supplies to the Mujihadeen.

TWO

THE HEAVY WOODEN door of the tenement block where the taxi deposited him was locked. With its cast-iron fenestration and carved stone reliefs, the building had obviously been a superior dwelling, not a working-class tenement. On the wall were buzzers for each flat. He ran his eye down the list of occupants till he read *Unterbringung der Humboldt Universität*. He pressed. Nothing happened. He pressed again and a buzz resulted. After a pause, unintelligible German competed with the crackling static. He uttered something which he hoped would convey his desire for entry. A long buzz was followed by a click and the door opened at his touch.

In the weak night-light, the wall tiles gleamed palely. From the lobby he ascended a steep stair with a carved banister. On the first floor the light went out and he had to feel his way along in the dark. A glimmer from above guided him on to an open door on the third floor where a woman disturbed from sleep stood slippered, curlered and wrapped in a dressing-gown. He attempted to explain himself but was brushed aside. '*Morgen, Morgen,*' was all she would say as she hustled him into the adjacent flat, showing him to a room at the end of a long corridor. Again he attempted to speak. Repeating her injunction to wait until the morrow, she handed him a set of keys, retreated and vanished.

Left alone, he contemplated the room. It was furnished in utilitarian decor of thin pine, reminding him of student residences he had known in the 1960s. There was a radio. In the corner was a glazed ceramic stove, tiled dark green, which was emitting vast amounts of heat. It presumably dated from the period of the building's construction, the turn of the century probably. Unable to reduce the stove's heat, he managed to open a window to the back-court after a struggle with the double-glazing.

Someone was playing a piano, or a record of a piano, somewhere in the block. Intensely cold air flooded into the room, taking the edge off the sulphurous smell of *Braunkohle* from the *Ofen*. As he inhaled the smell of coal, unfamiliar for decades, he identified the music as a Beethoven sonata, though he was unable to identify which one. Assuming that he must be exhausted, he went to bed. But with the heat of the stove and the swarming impressions of the day, sleep refused to come. His hours passed in little ease before he fell into a light sleep towards morning. He dreamed he had an appointment to meet someone at the waste land behind the Wall. Snow was falling. Behind him, mines exploded. People passed, unnoticing.

He had no alarm clock. At each waking, he leaned over to check the time on his watch at the bedside. At 6.30 he rose, washed and dressed. If there was anyone else in the apartment they were not yet stirring. The kitchen was empty and he had no provisions. A search of the fridge revealed a few items of food and some milk. They were fresh, so there was another occupant in the apartment, which he noted had three rooms.

To each according to his needs, he thought, helping himself to a glass of milk and a roll and cheese. He limited his depredations to the barely noticeable, making a mental note to replace them and to inform their proper owner in due course. There was no stir on the staircase and he tried to limit the noise from his tread as he descended to the street.

It was still not fully light. And again, bitterly cold. He glanced around; about a hundred yards away was a main thoroughfare, where *Strassenbahnen* were already scattering sparks from the iced overhead wires. Heading that way under the street lamps, he went in search of transport to the *Stadtmitte*, and the University.

He was in luck. As a tram rumbled to a stop, he pointed at it and asked a man waiting in the passenger shelter, '*Entschuldigung. Universität?*'

He received an affirmative nod and entered the vehicle, a single-decker with two carriages. He assumed he had heard the driver saying, '*Bitte einsteigen*', though it sounded like '*Beistei*' to his ears. His first encounter with *Berlinisch*. 'They don't speak German in Berlin,' he had been told, 'it's a different country.'

Then, panic. He had no money. It was illegal to take

Ostmarken either into or out of the country and he had arrived too late to exchange. But as there was no conductor, he decided to shrug off his first act of illegality in the state of *Real Existierende Sozialismus* as the ruling SED Party had recently designated it. Unhappily a passenger conveyed to him the need to stamp his ticket at a device provided.

'*Müss stempeln*,' insisted the law-abiding citizen.

In halting German, he conveyed his lack of a ticket and his lack of currency. A discussion amongst some of the passengers ensued, then one of them walked to the machine, stamped a ticket of his own and handed it to the foreign traveller with a smile. Legalities had been observed. Profuse with thanks, he accepted the ticket, which had been the cause of the international incident. On examination, it proved to be worth two pence. He decided to keep it as a memento to his avoidance of illegality on this occasion.

The journey was long and slow, down wide avenues divided in the centre by the overhead *U-Bahn*. He scanned his city plan, and then what he could see outside the window, for any point of correspondence. He was able to locate Dimitroffstrasse station on the map, after passing it in the tram, but lost his bearings again in the Prenzlauer Berg, an area of nineteenth-century working-class tenements.

Many shops, he noted, still bore the old-style lacquered shop signs. On a little further and he passed some large buildings, either museums or government offices, indicating that they were approaching the city centre. On one building undergoing restoration there was an inscription behind the scaffolding. Though the letters had been removed, the bolt holes and the lighter stone underneath made it quite legible. He translated to himself, 'William II, by God's grace Kaiser.' The shadow of the past, banal and obvious as it might be, that the DDR could not jump over, any more that he could vault his own.

He decided to descend, to walk and then to seek directions. A sweeper was cleaning an already spotless street with a small electric vehicle in which he sat. In answer to his request he received instructions, which he was able to follow more by the motions of the sweeper's arms than by those of his lips. It was now full day and the pavements glistened with rime. He came upon an open square fronting a large church: St Hedwig's. This was Bebelplatz, formerly Opernplatz, the wall plaque stated. Here he knew, 'un-German' books carried from the University Library had been burned after Hitler came to power. Already he was tripping over history at street corners. Behind every material object lay the past; a significant past. Here history had happened, swept all along in its tidal wave. On his little island, a few bits of flotsam and jetsam, a few pieces of near-history were all that had been deposited by the benign Gulf Stream of its past.

Raising his eyes from the cobbles of Bebelplatz, he saw a building in the classical Prussian style of architecture, flanked by two stone sentry boxes. Crossing to the gate between them, across a wide avenue, which another sign indicated was the Unter den Linden, he entered the

University grounds and halted. Here Hegel had lectured on the philosophy of history, arguing that previous forms of consciousness could not be restored. Here the youthful and pre-materialist Marx had written poems to Jenny. Here Bismarck had completed his studies, after being expelled from Hanover.

And now, he himself had come.

Sandy flower beds flanked the path to the main entrance. Here the material on which Prussia was built – sand – showed through, when it was not cobbled or concreted over; sand was visible too on the walls of the courtyard where the harling had flaked off to show crumbling brick underneath. First Prussia, and now the DDR, had little better materials to build with.

As he had been directed, he crossed the vast polished entrance hall and ascended a wide staircase, below a bust of Liebknecht, the communist leader murdered in 1919. Stopping to read the inscription, he discovered that he too had studied here. Down a long, echoing corridor, clean and austere, he found the office where he had been told to report. Inside sat a typist, working at a machine that looked like the gilded cast-metal typewriter he himself used at home. Both probably dated from the middle part of the century.

He asked for Dr Feld. And waited.

Scargill Prophet of Doom

Arthur Scargill, recently-elected President of the National Union of Mineworkers, expressed his "regret" that the members of his union had voted narrowly to accept a below-inflation pay award of 9.3% from the National Coal Board. Mr. Scargill predicted that this would only be the first of a series of cuts in the real wages of miners, and would be followed by Conservative government plans to "butcher" the coal industry, reducing the work force to 75,000 from its present level of nearly 300,000. Government and Coal Board spokesmen said that Mr. Scargill's claims were scaremongering and were based on fantasy, adding that the coal industry had a bright future.

CHAPTER THREE

DR FELD – THE WOMAN who had met him at Friedrichstrasse station – emerged from her office, greeted him and began to organise him. This was pleasant and welcome after his journey. She bustled with the secretary, who produced forms and stamps from her desk and looked slightly displeased that her desultory typing had been interrupted. He was handed one piece of stamped paper, along with 20 marks.

'*Stipendium.*'

As he was assimilating the sight of Marx and Engels on the currency, he was handed another paper,

'*Bibliothekskarte.*'

He had to sign them both, and then for them both, under the watchful eyes, like a child obeying instructions. The bureaucratic formalities complete, he entered Dr Feld's office. This was again austere. Books lined one wall; utility chairs another. In the centre was a massive, littered desk. She sat, motioning him to sit also.

'So,' she opened, '*Sie kommen Bismarck zu studieren,*' and waited for him to explain himself.

To enable him to visit the DDR, he had devised a historiographical project, which caught the imagination of the Cultural Mission. He attempted to explain it in his passable, though long unused, German. The DDR was a country without a history, having rejected the history of Germany and Prussia as a great misery. But having existed for over three decades, it had to face the problem of a national territorial heritage. As most of the present DDR was the old Mark Brandenburg, the core of historical Prussia, coming to terms with Prussia was the central problem. He wanted to investigate DDR historical writing in this area.

She listened attentively to what he had to say, then smiled, inclining her head.

'You want to give us a territorial tradition?' she suggested.

He replied that no country could totally reject its territorial traditions; it was necessary to look at the past as Marx had done, as a mixture of good and bad, or rather progressive and reactionary, elements.

'Here you have not done that. Bismarck, for example. Your writers say that he was always reactionary, but Marx says he was revolutionary in uniting Germany.'

Being on familiar ground made his German flow more fluently. Talking about the ostensible reason for his trip, pushed uncertainty about the real reason from his mind.

She prevaricated.

'Yes, there is a lot of historical discussion in our

country now about the "revolution from above" and the "revolution from below"...'

In full flight now, as she watched him he continued, 'But the "revolution from below" was not possible at that time. Last month Frederick the Great's statue was replaced on the Unter den Linden, after you had kept it in storage for thirty years. If the Bismarck *Denkmal* had been here and not in West Berlin, what would you have done with it?'

Her slight ironic smile, the smile of the Mitropa waiter on the train, widened before she gave her reply.

'As you say, we have fortunately been spared that problem. And I do not really know. I am not an expert on German Unification, the Reformation is my field. It is easy however, to be objective about a period, or a country, where you do not live. And with us these things are important.'

Bei uns sind diese Sachen wichtig.

He repeated her words to himself as she looked at her watch and then brought their interview to an end.

'Come, I must soon lecture, but before I will show you the library.'

She led him back along the linoleum-floored corridor to the main library, thence through a turnstile where a sign announced *'Sektion Geschichte'*. His fate was removed from his hands as Dr Feld talked with a young librarian, who gave him quizzical looks, mixed with smiles, over the older woman's shoulder. As Dr Feld left, she instructed the scholar to come and see her again once he had made his preliminary enquiries.

The librarian, smiling engagingly, led him down yet

another corridor, to a dimly lit room. From the rows of similar bindings on the shelves, he assumed it was the periodicals section; it looked as unused as in any University. She pointed to a desk raised on a dais, overlooking a street he could already identify as Unter den Linden.

'*Hier. Für Sie.*'

Apparently he was to have sole use of this during his stay. She patiently explained that each day he must fill out his requests for materials; the next morning these would be on his desk, waiting for him. He expressed polite satisfaction with the arrangements and looked around.

His eye caught a faded map, locating the place of publication of all the periodicals in the room. He stopped in surprise. The map was of Germany in 1937, showing the pre-1914 frontiers.

He pointed to it in surprise and said, '*Diese Karte zeigt die alten Grenzen.*'

The librarian looked suddenly uninterested and offered with a shrug, '*Ja, ja. Alte Karte, alte Grenzen.*' Then she gave him a lacklustre smile and bade him goodbye.

He stood until the footfall ceased. Then, at random, he picked up a volume. It was the *Statistisches Jahrbuch für das Deutsche Reich* of 1894. Inside the front cover had been stamped a swastika; it had been inefficiently scratched out and replaced by the hammer and compass logo of the DDR. Glancing through other periodicals, he noted that this was a general feature, betraying a surprising lack of attention to detail. Or almost a consciousness of impermanence. Like the map, he thought.

He spent a couple of hours looking up references he had made prior to his visit.

The sound of music floated to his ears; he walked to the window and stared out. In the street was a detachment of the *Volksarmee*, a brass band unit, playing a tune that reminded him of 'Knees Up, Mother Brown'. Directly in front of the window, in the centre of the Unter den Linden stood Rauch's bronze statue of Frederick the Great, which he had mentioned to Dr Feld. Everything was becoming unreal, he was being pursued by symbols and ironies at every turn. He wondered if Dr Feld had instructed the librarian to give him that seat; yes, he was sure she had. He decided to break the semi-surreal spell that was enveloping him and leave off study till the next day. Hastily filling in some requests for materials, he left them on the librarian's desk. She did not look up as he went.

'Material reality, food,' he thought, having not eaten more than a stolen mouthful since the train, the day before. The day before? Already it seemed like months ago. He retraced his steps to the foot of the staircase and looked around.

A tide of people was moving past and as it was midday he decided to follow them to see if that way lay a meal. A queue at a ticket kiosk confirmed his hunch and he joined it. A menu on the wall indicated fare and prices. He bought tickets for soup, bread and fruit.

The canteen reminded him of those in factories where he had worked in the days when he sought physical contact with the proletariat. It was spartan, and full. He joined the queue for food and received a large bowl of *Erbsensuppe* with a chunk of rye bread. At the end of the counter a stony-faced woman stood between a bucket of bruised apples and a basin of semi-blackened bananas. He pointed to the banana. She shook her head and pointed to the bucket.

'*Apfel*,' she intimated.

He took an apple, which turned out to be sweet despite the bruising. The students, well-ordered and quiet, unfailingly took their dirty dishes back to the service hatch. As he sat, a shaft of sunlight drew a line on his table; looking up, he saw that the sun had come out and was streaming in through the windows of the roof. Disposing of his dishes he went out onto the courtyard, where students sat talking or reading on stone benches in the sun. He almost felt rejuvenated, a student himself again, the world full of unresolved issues which he was confident his intellect would unravel – rather than merely compounding their irresolution.

Between the sentry boxes he stood uncertain as to his direction, east or west. But his attention was taken up by a crowd on his left, to the eastward, where he turned. Joining the crowd, he found they were waiting for the changing of the guard at the building he knew from pictures was Schinkel's *Neue Wache*, now the Memorial to the Victims of Fascism and Militarism. Here Hitler had laid wreaths for Stalingrad. Fresh-faced, immaculate, impassive young guards changed places, executing the Prussian goose-step. Another detail, like the library map, left over from the past. The crowd then dispersed, largely to tourist buses which bore West Berlin number plates. Inside, the eternal flame burned inside a cut glass plinth; 'To the Unknown Resistance Fighter' was the dedication.

Next he walked the short distance westwards to

Rauch's memorial to *Der alte Fritz* in the middle of the street and looked up at the old misanthrope's face, its bitterness contrasting with the grace of the statue. Round the plinth were bas-reliefs of Frederick's military campaigns and commanders. On the off-chance he looked, hoping to find a reference to Marshall Keith, one of Frederick's commanders. Keith, who hailed from his own cold and barren North-East Scotland, had come as a soldier of fortune, to cold and barren Prussia – and there he was, relieving the siege of Stralsund. Maybe he himself would relieve his own siege on this trip.

As he continued westwards down the Unter den Linden, he noticed the architecture change from restored Prussian classicism to functional 1950s glass and concrete, low-slung to keep the line of the street. On his left lay the massive monolith of the Soviet Embassy.

The street ended. Over beyond the Wall fluttered a German flag on what he assumed was the Reichstag Building in West Berlin. The tops of those trees over there must be the *Tiergarten*, he thought. Beyond that was the bifurcated rump of the Pariser Platz, which ended in the Wall. But before the Wall, in splendid isolation, was the Brandenburger Tor, its lower sections occupied by the *Grenzpolizei*.

He wondered how far he could go, and walked on. One of the *Grenzpolizei* approached him, eyed him carefully, and held out a hand.

'*Nicht weiter. Nicht gestattet.*'

He nodded to signify comprehension and asked if he could photograph the *Brandenburger Tor*. The border guard shrugged in indifferent agreement as he resumed his perambulations. The scholar-become-photographer then resumed his walk back to the University and crossed the *Marx-Engels Brücke* over the Spree to Karl Liebknecht Strasse, where he awaited his transport home. Checking the timetable at the stop, he saw he had twenty minutes to wait for the tram.

To kill time he entered an Intershop which lay nearby. After having his passport checked, he wandered round the aisles of goods available for hard currency. There were Western luxury goods, perfumes, alcohol and other items not available in state shops here, and also DDR goods like cameras. There was also junk: cheap Western car stickers, kitschy block-mounted prints and Western brands of washing powder all at what seemed to him ridiculous prices. He asked the shelf stacker, pointing to these goods, whether anybody bought them.

'*Ja, ja, natürlich.*'

On his way back he felt a little more familiar with the scene; the crowded tenements of Prenzlauer Berg, the broad avenues leading north to Pankow, where he lived. Familiar with the door switch this time, he made the ascent to his flat without incident. Dishes in the sink confirmed that there was another occupant. And reminded him of his own lack of provisions. He would go looking for something to eat later.

Unlocking his door, he found that the bed had been made and the window opened. In the back court of the tenement square there were allotments and a children's playpark. The cold air from outside mingled with the heat from the *Ofen*, which had been lit. He greeted it as a familiar friend. He closed the window, hung up his coat and sat down to write home. Words flowed easily from his pen: he had always found writing easier than speaking. He re-read what he had written, folded the letter into an envelope and sealed it.

Rising Birth-rate Signals Strength

Statistics recently released show that the birth rate in our Republic has attained its highest level for many decades, with new births greatly outstripping deaths. This, along with the increasing return to the country of citizens who had previously decided to leave the D.D.R., means that for the first time in many years, the country has reached a satisfactory state of population dynamics.

These facts and figures show the great confidence that our citizens have in the stability, security and prosperity offered by life in the D.D.R., which increasingly contrasts favourably with the superficially glamorous but crisis-ridden and insecure world offered by capitalism, and specifically by the B.R.D. with its mounting unemployment, homelessness and crime.

CHAPTER FOUR

HE WENT OVER to the table and switched on the radio. After running the tuner along the full length of the waveband, he found a jazz programme. When the music stopped, the announcer stated that it was a broadcast from the US Armed Forces Network, Berlin. The English startled him. A record in memoriam Thelonious Monk, who had recently died, followed. He wondered why the US broadcasts were not jammed, then listened to the music for a while. At 7 the AFN News interrupted the jazz:

> *Soviet forces in Afghanistan appear to have suffered a major setback in a battle with Afghan freedom fighters at the Salang Tunnel in the north of the country. Reports indicate...*

He decided to go out in search of food. As he entered the lobby he noticed, before he switched on the light, that there was a light under the door of the room next to his. Presumably the flatmate whose stores he had raided. As he descended the stairs, he was greeted by a young neighbour with a child. He returned the greeting. The chill outside air made him hurry to the junction between two broad avenues which intersected about twenty yards from the doorstep of the *Unterbringung*.

The first window to show a light appeared to be a cafe frequented by youngsters. He decided it was not what he was looking for. Further on, a red neon sign announced *Ratskeller*. Outside was a menu of enormous length and, as he quickly calculated, great cheapness. He descended the stairs into the warmth and was heading for the restaurant when a voice halted him. He turned.

'*Garderobe*,' the trim cloakroom attendant repeated impassively and he deduced that he had to hand over his coat. She took it, looked at it, probably knowing from it that he was 'from the capitalist exterior', for it was made of real leather which here was generally seen only on the backs of *Grenzpolizei* and *Vopos* – and he was obviously neither.

'*Zwanzig Pfennig*.'

He handed over the money, took a ticket and entered the restaurant, a large establishment with thirty or forty tables, mostly unoccupied at this relatively early hour. He picked a table and studied the menu. There seemed to be nothing that was not available; it looked like the index of a cookery manual. The waitress arrived and divided her time between giving him a cocky look and flirting with a waiter.

As he pointed to the menu she interrupted, '*Nein,*

nein. Tagesmenü,' and pointed to a chalked wall-board displaying a more restricted choice of fare.

He made his order and she moved off immediately, asking over her shoulder: '*Und Bier?*'

He nodded, then began to look around at his fellow diners. At the next table were an old couple having a quiet beer. A young man in a leather jacket sat alone. At the far wall was a family party whose dress and demeanour suggested some form of celebration.

The waitress came back and served his food. It was not what he had ordered. He pointed this out, reminding her of his order.

'*Ausverkauft,*' she replied pertly, leaving him with what must have been *Kalbsbraten mit Sauerkraut,* as he worked out from the *Tagesmenü* by a process of elimination. As he ate and drank, he watched the floor-show of the waitress flirting with the waiter and the male diners.

As she passed his table he said, '*Noch ein Bier bitte.*'

She cheekily asked if he had enjoyed his food. He replied that he had; this and his other comments had revealed that he was foreign. The old couple looked towards him.

The young man in the leather jacket rose, and carrying over his beer, asked, '*Ist dieser Platz noch frei?*'

The scholar indicated that it was. The young man sat down and began to talk earnestly. Where are you from? What are you doing in the DDR? What are your impressions of the country? He listened intently to the answers he received, as if cataloguing them mentally.

Should I be worried that this man is a police spy?

the scholar thought. But worry would not come and he asked questions in return. The young man had just returned from the Soviet Union, he said, where he had been working on the Urengoy gas pipeline, of which the DDR was building a section. This work had enabled him to earn enough to buy a car and to move up the housing list on his return. Besides, to be involved with the project was his 'internationalist duty' in the light of the boycott of the pipeline imposed by the US imperialists after the Soviet intervention in Afghanistan.

'And it is good to do something big once in your life,' he added.

The beer had begun to produce a mellow tipsiness in the scholar. He thought, this seems so much a set-up, it has to be genuine. And then, yes, something big once in your life...

His new friend offered to get more beer and he agreed.

By this time the couple at the next table had awoken to the discussion and leaned over to participate in it. The restaurant was filling up. Behind them, four *Volkspolizisten* had entered and were ordering a meal.

The old man spoke in simulated pidgin German.

'*Pivo gut*, Russian soldiers say *Pivo gut*.'

The scholar politely concurred in praising the quality of the local beer. The old man pulled his chair closer.

'You are studying in Berlin. You must be a Communist Party member?'

He indicated that he was not. That his was an academic study, relating to Bismarck.

'Ah, Bismarck. *Siegesäule*.' The old man frowned.

'West Berlin. I have not been there since '61. I would like to go again. You can go, but for me it is not possible. They put up the Wall to stop people going there.' Then, matter-of-factly, '*Hier in der* DDR *haben wir keine wirkliche Freiheit.*'

His wife gave him a nudge and inclined her head slightly towards the *Volkspolizisten*. The old man shrugged, unconcerned. The police paid no attention.

'But we have no homelessness or unemployment either; there is plenty of both in West Berlin,' commented the former gas pipeline worker. 'We had to close the border to stop smuggling. Even now they would come with their Deutschmarks and buy everything up if we let them. And most of those who left were Nazis or other enemies of socialism, whom we did not want anyway. And look, have you seen *Neues Deutschland* today...? It is full of interviews with returnees, people who have found life is not so wonderful over there. Look, read it for yourself.'

But the old man was not interested in a political discussion and did not accept the proffered newspaper. He switched, in his nasal *Berlinisch*, to extolling the virtues of Pankow and its sights. '*Zu Beishel,*' he kept saying when giving an example of another sight that must be seen. The scholar promised to visit the local *Schloss* and the medieval *Kirche*, which assurances seemed to give the old man pleasure. But exhaustion from his sleepless night finally forced the scholar to take his leave. This was only achieved after an extended formality of shaking the hand of everyone he had talked to whilst in the place. Collecting his coat, he ascended back into the winter night. He stood breathing in the night air when the old couple from the restaurant emerged beside him. The old man nodded back towards the restaurant and warned, '*Vorsicht!*' and nodding again, added, '*Stasi,*' before departing.

A short walk took the scholar home, where he prepared for bed. When he was half undressed all the lights went out. He fumbled his way to the lobby and struggled to adjust his eyes to the dark, then started. There was someone else in the corridor, somewhere near him. He could hear faint breathing, then heard his own. He stared into the darkness, straining to hear and see.

'*Was ist denn los? Was ist denn los?*'

From the end of the lobby came a voice that he recognised as that of the caretaker, Frau Hügeln. The front door of the flat had been opened and this allowed a weak light from the stairwell to enter, enabling him to make out from the indistinct outline, that his companion in the dark was a woman. A torch showed at the end of the corridor and its beam played across his face and chest, and then lit up another face heavy with sleep and with large eyes that stared at him. The girl stood in her nightdress, he in his underpants, while the beam played over them.

'*Ah so,*' said Frau Hügeln, arms on hips. She had jumped to an understandable conclusion. The girl said nothing. A stream of unintelligible invective came from the caretaker, more for show than heartfelt, he thought. The caretaker worked at what was presumably the fuse box at the end of the corridor; the lights went on again. Then Frau Hügeln brushed past them into the girl's bedroom, detaching electrical appliances from their sockets, doing the same afterwards in the kitchen.

'*Zu viel, zu viel!*' she scolded, explaining that the circuit must not be overloaded. She stopped then, looked at them both fixedly with what seemed like the ghost of a smile, the Mitropa smile. Then, roughly, '*Jetz gehe ich.*'

The front door closed behind her and they stood awkward and silent in the light. Then the girl said in what he recognised was not native German, '*Es ist so kalt. Ich habe keinen Ofen.*'

He had the unreal feeling of being an actor in a bad film. He muttered something appropriate and moved back to his room. It seemed an age till he heard her door close.

He poured himself a whisky, a Talisker; he did not travel well without the wine of his own country. And its price here was prohibitive, so he had brought a bottle. Sipping it, he thought of this and other occasions in the past. Always the gentleman. He switched on the radio and tuned it till something acceptable filled the silence. He sipped his drink and listened to the same programme on Thelonious Monk that US Forces Radio had been playing when he had gone out. It was a long tribute. The music went well with the whisky and with his mood.

The door was knocked. He considered not answering. It was knocked again. He went and opened it.

His flatmate was still in her nightdress, but she appeared to have combed her hair. She was holding an empty cup, as if asking for, or offering, a libation.

'*Haben Sie Zucker?*' she asked, and waited.

He thought of those occasions when hesitation had snatched the cup and its sweet contents from him in the past. But now he had crossed an emotional frontier, he was slipping away from himself. He was in moral hibernation. The words came to him easily this time.

'*Nein. Aber ich habe Whisky. Wollen Sie trinken?*'

She smiled, '*Ja,*' and entered, bringing her cup.

Petrol Bombs Thrown in Bristol Riot

Violent disturbances broke out in the St. Paul's district of Bristol last night. In scenes reminiscent of last summer's serious riots there and other inner city areas such as Moss Side in Manchester, Toxteth in Liverpool and Brixton in London, gangs of youths roamed the streets erecting makeshift barricades and throwing petrol bombs at the police.

The situation became so serious that the police were forced to withdraw, leaving St. Paul's in the hands of the rioters, who went on a trail of destruction and looting. Conservative M.P.s have blamed the riots on the black community and called for tighter immigration controls and repatriation. Community leaders, however, cite the police as saying that as many white as black youths took part in the riots, and state that unemployment, deprivation and police harassment are the cause of the problems.

CHAPTER FIVE

IN THE MORNING he woke to a half-empty bed and a three-quarters empty whisky bottle. He went to the toilet to wash. Pushing aside a string of women's washing hanging in the shower, he switched on the water. It was scalding. He washed moving in and out of the flow, unable to discover how to regulate the temperature.

Drying himself, he walked into the kitchen. There was a cup and plate in the sink. He felt, in return for his whisky, entitled to raid the provisions in the fridge for his breakfast now. He drank his flatmate's coffee and ate her *Schwarzbrot*.

With a feeling of familiarity he descended to the street, mounted the *Strassenbahn* and like an old hand obtained his ticket and stamped it. From the front of the queue a coin was passed down and given to him, to purchase a ticket for a fellow passenger. He tore off a ticket and handed it back. But his neighbour politely refused it, pointing. '*Sie müssen stempeln*,' he smiled.

So he stamped it and the ticket made its way back down the line to the coin's former owner.

The tram passed down an avenue with neat flowerbeds, bushes and shrubs pruned against the coming spring on either side. They bore legends: *Verschönert Unsere Hauptstadt Berlin! Alles für das Wohl des Volkes und das Glück der Kinder!* Politics in flower beds. Outside the tenements of Prenzlauer Berg, lorries were depositing piles of *Braunkohle* beside the grilles over the basements. He knew now not to get off here but to wait till the tram had crossed the Spree and reached Am Kupfergraben. He was in no hurry and went to the canteen for a coffee before starting work. He noticed many of the students were reading or writing as they drank. He could take his time: there was no haste over what he had to do.

In the periodicals room a small stove near his desk had been lit. Beside it was a bucket of *Braunkohle* nuts. The room was overheated, the radiators were also on, and so he opened the window. Old Fritz scowled down from his horse at the cars moving along the Unter den Linden. There were a few Western cars. Most were Russian Ladas or local Trabbis, which coughed asthmatically in the chill air when they started. On his desk, neatly stacked, were the books he had requested and a fresh pile of request slips printed on thin paper. He set to work.

His problem was the dichotomy between desire and reality, the dialectic of what was objectively possible and subjectively desirable. *Realpolitik*, as Bismarck had put it. Bismarck had united Germany by force and militaristic methods; DDR writers, rejecting everything Prussian, argued that this was reactionary and that a popular democratic revolution should have united Germany.

Could, should, he thought. Less than a syllable of difference. His task, which had enthused the mandarins of the Cultural Mission, was to see if Prussia was being rehabilitated and its cultural and historical traditions being claimed as the DDR's own. He worked through till lunchtime, then went to the canteen where he ate observing those around him, but speaking to no one. He was freeing himself from the mesh of normal relations, floating. No one knew him or expected anything of him. He was getting to like the feeling.

He was obliged to report to the Cultural Mission on arrival and had omitted to do so on the previous day. So he decided to go there after lunch, report and post home the letter he had written the previous evening – which he did not want to go via DDR mail. It was again a cold day and he breathed the invigoratingly crisp air as he walked the short distance to the Mission. For a decade now, Her Britannic Majesty's Government had recognised the Democratic Republic, accepted the existence of two Germanies as something fixed. The Berlin Wall was as permanent as the Great Wall of China, everyone knew that now.

Outside the Mission, a small cluster of people looked into one of the windows facing the Unter den Linden. A display showed Charles and Diana, like the actualisation of a prince and princess from Grimms' tales, at various functions in the Thatcherland calender. In the other window on the far side of the entrance was housed another display, 'Britain Today'. It was, it appeared, a land of quaint local customs performed by happy country folk. The police wore strange hats and always smiled. Black people lived there and appeared to be fun-loving. The sun generally shone. There was no Brixton, no steel strike, no dole queues. No one lived in cardboard cities, as they did in that other country he had just come from. He studied the locals, themselves studying the photographs; they looked a little quizzical and bemused. He wondered what impression they took away as to the benefits of the democratic system. But he could detect a certain fascination in the attention they gave to the pictures. He thought of the old man in the pub last night and his obsession with West Berlin.

At the information counter, the groomed secretary told him that the Director would be down presently, would he like to take a seat? The tables were spread with the colour supplements of the Sunday newspapers. He glanced at some, laid them aside and waited.

Again, as he saw the Director moving towards him, he felt that the ham director of this drama he felt himself to be in was guilty of typecasting. The man was tall and slim in his striped suit, with regulation Oxbridge accent and confidence oozing from every pore. He was also very young.

'Ah, yes, Dr...' he said as he proffered his hand. It was warm and soft.

'Mr,' he corrected.

'Yes, Mr... So, well, you're Prussia, eh? Not my line, really. But did you hear about the stushie, eh? With the statue? Did you read about it in *The Times*?'

He replied that he had seen a report on the DDR leader

Honecker's speech about the restoration of Frederick the Great's statue to its former location on the Unter den Linden, in the *Guardian*.

'The *Guardian*, eh?' commented the Director, as if this was a significant piece of information, 'Yes, well…'

After a pause he continued, 'No trouble so far with these chappies? Should be all right, but they can be, well… you know what I mean? It's a bit, well, you know, it's not like home. Example: I've been trying to get a piano for months. Play a bit. Can't get one… they're all for export.' He waved a mildly deprecating hand.

'I don't think I'll be needing a piano.'

'Eh? No, I don't suppose so.'

The scholar asked if he could use the Mission mail and proffered the letter.

The Director appeared delighted.

'No problem, glad we can be of help. Goes every day to London with the West Berlin Forces mail. The local post can be a bit… unreliable, shall we say. No inviolability of the mail over here! They may not send you to the gulag any more, but it's still not democratic by any means.' There was a prolonged, rather awkward pause before the Director continued, 'But look, once you've settled down a bit, done a bit of work, you know, we might organise something with some of the locals, eh? International cultural co-operation and all that?'

The scholar said yes and rose to go, briefly shaking the proffered, scented hand.

It had been an unpleasant wrench out of hibernation and he wanted to leave.

The Director watched him depart. Once the scholar

had left the building, the official went behind the reception desk and said to the secretary sitting there, 'Get me security, please.'

He was put through. 'I've a letter coming your way, and I want to know what's in it. Also, checks on the content of all mail coming in for Dr...' he smiled, 'Sorry, Mr...'

He replaced the receiver. 'Silly chappie,' he murmured as he stared towards the exit.

The secretary looked up from behind her desk; she was filing a rag-nail.

'What's going on with that fellow?'

The Director smiled conspiratorially and tapped his nose.

'Time I was moving on from Berlin. This fellow is going to be my means of exit.'

'I don't understand. Why don't you ask for a transfer?' She examined the filed nail.

'Oh no. That wouldn't do. Wouldn't do at all. You see, I want to leave under a cloud. This laddie is foolish enough to provide me, hopefully, with the means.'

'I'm still not with you.' Another angle of the nail was examined.

'Well, and of course this is all hush-hush, we want to expel one of their chaps from London, the Cultural Attaché. Got nothing on him, though. But if I get removed, I'll be an innocent diplomat persecuted by the wicked communists, and tit for tat we can get rid of this chap in London, who, unlike my humble, cultural self, is engaged in "activities incompatible with his diplomatic position".'

'But what has that to do with our scholar?' She seemed pleased with the nail now and began to repair its varnish.

'Hmm,' the Director mused, 'he's one of these idealists. Thinks the DDR isn't awful because it's Communist, but because it's not "pure" enough for his liking – God forbid! He's silly enough to serve our purpose, as long as he's seen around with me a bit. The "other side" will notice that, they'll be keeping tabs on him. They think all Cultural Mission scholars are spies.'

'But what will happen to him?' She blew on the nail.

'To him? Happen to him?' The Director seemed surprised at the question. 'Nothing much, I suppose. In the old days they sent you to the salt mines, but now they just tend to dump you over the border on a one-way ticket if you annoy them. People wanting to defect have found it is easier if you turn up at Alexanderplatz with a protest placard, rather than trying to get over that bloody Wall and through the minefields.'

Solidarity Marchers Clash with Police

Clashes took place today between police and demonstrators in Warsaw and other cities. The biggest battle took place in Gdansk, stronghold of the Solidarity trades union. 10,000 people marched through the city after laying flowers at the spot where workers were shot dead in the 1970 protests. When the crowd made for the Communist Party Headquarters, set alight in 1970, police turned on water cannons and fired tear gas grenades. A message from the Pope stressed the need to avoid violence, but called for the Polish government to recognise basic trades union rights in the country.

CHAPTER SIX

DESCENDING FROM THE TRAM in Pankow a stop early, he eyed the red brick *Kirche* beside the stop. A plaque dated it as thirteenth century. He tried the door handle, it was locked. Across the road was the *Kaufhalle*, whose sign he had noted when passing that morning in the *Strassenbahn*. He crossed over to it. He would keep his promise to the old man and look at the church another time.

The street was lined with shops of a variety he had not expected in the Stalinist Sparta. A game and poultry shop, a milliner's, a hairdresser's, a couple of cafes and a *Delikatessen*. The supermarket was like the smaller ones that had opened in Britain in the 1960s, built for pedestrian shoppers, not motorists. As he walked round, he eyed the shelves. There seemed to be little that was unavailable, though there were no special offers, and limited variety... one kind of soap powder, one brand of butter... at the fruit and vegetable counter there was also a limited choice. Potatoes, turnip, carrots, piles of the sweet and battered apples he had already tasted – and '*Orangen aus Kuba*', as the sign above the counter proclaimed. And a mountain of pineapples. He noticed that everyone bought one, some people bought several; one man's trolley was full of them. He wondered idly what barter deal with what African country had led to the pineapple glut. He made his few purchases of milk, bread, coffee and butter. At the counter, no plastic bags – everyone carried their own shopping bags, just as his mother had done when dragging him to the shops when he was a child. So his pockets were requisitioned for transporting some of the purchases and he carried the rest. Walking along the now dark streets, he wondered what he would find at the flat; wondered what he wanted to find.

His room door was unlocked, which was convenient as his arms were burdened. She sat reading on the bed. Looking up, she said, '*Mir war kalt. Hier ist es wärmer.*'

She spoke the words confidently, yet there was a hint of unease on her features afterwards. He had locked the door on leaving and wondered, felt he should ask how she had got in but decided not to. He did not want to know. He deposited his purchases and indicated that he was going to make coffee for them both. On bringing it back, he was aware that something was expected of him, some response to her presence. She was watching him. He looked over at her, made his decision.

'We can go out to eat tonight somewhere. Would you like to?'

It seemed an inadequate, evasive response to the situation but she broke into a smile and agreed. She went back to her room to get ready, leaving him drinking his coffee. As he drank he felt in the presence of a *fait accompli*. Something was happening to him and he had missed his chance to prevent it. He poured a little of what was left of the Talisker into a glass and sipped it as he waited.

On her return, he was surprised. Like all students here, she dressed in the androgynous jeans and jumpers that had been uniform in his own student days in the 1960s. But now she had made up her large eyes and donned a dress that looked as if it had been bought with *Westmarks* in one of the Intershops on the Unter den Linden.

'*Wohin?*' he asked, with what he realised were rising good spirits, and finished the whisky. He would have to drink the local spirit now, his own exhausted after only two days.

Instead of replying, she took his hand and skipped energetically as she led him downstairs and outside. They walked in the direction of the tram halt but she detached herself from him and flagged down a taxi.

'*Zu kalt um zu warten,*' she smiled conspiratorially and then, confidently, to the driver, '*Ermeler Haus, Märkishes Ufer.*'

In the comfort of the cab beside this young woman whose name he did not yet know, he looked out at the dark city, which he also did not know. It was a pleasant feeling. He was enjoying winter; being warm within seemingly secure walls.

The taxi stopped by the Spree – Märkishes Ufer, he read, as they got out. A row of restored eighteenth-century patrician houses faced them, their frontages painted in pastel colours. Between an antiquarian bookshop and an art dealer was a small cast-iron sign announcing the Ermeler Haus, which was further designated as a *HOG Gaststätte* of 'exceptional quality'. Inside the restored roccoco facade glittered chandeliers. A waiter in formal attire approached them over the thick carpet. When they requested a table, he frigidly informed them that the restaurant was fully booked. The scholar was about to go, but his companion held his sleeve and continued to talk to the waiter, then turned to him and asked: 'Can you pay in Westmarks or dollars? Pounds? That is not so good, but it will do.' And they were admitted. After the ritual of the *Garderobe*, she explained, 'They will pay the bill themselves in Ostmarks and use the foreign currency in the Intershops, where Ostmarks are not allowed.'

He remarked that denying DDR citizens the right to buy in certain shops was hardly an example of good socialist practice. She looked at him fixedly. Then broke into a smile, the Mitropa smile again. 'But it is still the realm of necessity here and not the realm of freedom. A transitional phase,' and she pulled him by the hand, upstairs to the dining room.

It was the kind of place he would have had hesitated before entering in the West – partly because of the clientele over there, partly because of the price. He studied the ornate plasterwork ceiling and damasked walls, crystal and porcelain on the tables, the waiters in formal dress in attendance. Ermeler Haus had been the residence of a merchant prince of the time of Frederick the Great and was restored as a restaurant after the war, announced a framed placard on the wall. They were led to a table overlooking an enclosed garden courtyard. He looked around at their fellow diners.

Across from them sat a large, official-looking group, possibly Party functionaries. A group of girls were having what appeared to be a hen-night. They were noisy, by German standards. And a young couple in jeans sat next to them. Finally, audible as well as visible, were two US military personnel, evidently of high rank, from the paragraphs of braid on their shoulders, accompanied by women who looked much younger, dazzling with lip gloss and nail varnish.

His companion saw him looking at the Americans, then volunteered in an offhand way, 'They come here because for them it is very cheap to eat, and then they go to the opera, which is also not expensive. After, they can go home and say from experience how awful communism is. They have the right to come here at any time under the agreement for the occupation of Berlin.'

'And they also come here because here no one will see them with women who are not their wives,' he added, a little disapprovingly.

'Like you,' she said, with a minxish incline of her head, enjoying his embarrassment. 'And for you too it will not be expensive. People in the West are all very rich, I hear.'

He began to feel annoyed at his own passivity, restive at being played with; he wanted to take some initiative. All he could muster, however, was a flat-sounding, 'Why did you come to the DDR?'

She was Bulgarian, she said, also on exchange at the University, studying hydraulics.

He noticed that the wine they were drinking was, by

coincidence, Bulgarian – *Bärenblut*.

'*Langweilig*,' she said, pursing up her face, 'but that way I can get some money and travel. Bulgaria is very boring, nothing but loganberries, imagine! Russia is just as bad, I think. Here it is a little less boring, almost chic, eh? I would like to go to West Berlin, that must be very interesting. But it is not possible for me to travel in "capitalist foreign parts". You, from the West, must find it very dull here?'

He felt on the defensive, as if caught in an emotional chess game. She implied that her interest in him was because he was from the West and had Western currency. His real leather coat was a giveaway, she said.

'The coats here are not real leather, but *Kunstleder*.'

'I didn't have the coat on the first time you saw me. So that could not have been the attraction.'

Laughing, she spluttered on her wine. He had made a useful gambit. She aroused contrariness, petulance in him. And he had to admit, aroused great interest.

'Yes, it is dull here,' he continued. 'The tedium of not having advertising hoardings to look at is terrible. And in shops, to see toothpaste and soap powder not bearing the names of exotic plants or Greek heroes is dull. And it is dull to be here, in a place like this. In West Berlin I would be eating pizza or a McDonald's burger. I would have to, because that would be what I could afford. Not everyone in the West is rich. So there are some compensations here for the boredom.'

She looked at him sharply, without replying.

A waiter brought them their camembert with raspberry sauce. The silence between them continued till it was eaten. Then she raised her eyes to his.

'Why did you come to Berlin? Not to eat in luxury with American officers and have an affair – if you intend to have one – with a Bulgarian student?'

Fortuitously the main course arrived at that moment and as they were surrounded by waiters and waitresses serving the *gebratene Ente*, silence descended again. When only the wine on the table stood between them, he trotted out the speech he had made already to Dr Feld about his historical survey. Or a resumé of it.

'*Und nichts anders?*'

The question seemed to have a directness in German, or maybe that was just his imagination.

'No, nothing,' he replied, 'although what you said about the Bulgarian student sounds interesting.'

'I hope so,' she commented, staring at him quizzically, in what he took as a reference to the first, rather than the second part of his answer.

Then, with sudden cheerfulness and an engaging smile, she said, 'Come, since you cannot afford this at home, let us have more wine. And,' she added, lowering her voice, smiling her sweetest, well-practised smile, 'do you never ask the names of the young girls you sleep with?'

'That does not happen that often, I can assure you... and you did not ask my name either.'

'Yes, but I know yours. And mine is Marya. All Bulgarian girls are called Marya,' she laughed.

He took the bottle, poured the strong dark wine into his glass and drank. The same person was still writing the script of this melodrama, or farce. The label of the bottle caught his eye; a picture of a bear sleeping inside a tree.

Bears, he thought, hibernated in winter too. He poured again, wanting the wine quickly in his bloodstream.

The meal had cost him a week's *Stipendium*, but at twenty pounds all told he could see why dining at the Ermeler Haus appealed to the Americans. They walked along the Fischerinsel, past the scaffold-shrouded *Nikolaikirche* and soon he recognised ahead the Alexanderplatz, where he had asked directions of the street-sweeper. There were groups of youngsters around the fountain and the World Time Clock, scratched with tourist graffiti. The square was bordered on one side by the overhead *S-Bahn*.

As he made towards the *Eingang*, she stopped him and took his arm, said '*Noch nicht*,' and pulled him towards a glass-fronted kiosk inserted into the station wall. 'Mokka Bar', it read. Inside it was extremely cramped. The other customers, entirely male, stood knocking back schnapps, slivovic and tiny cups of black coffee. The air was thick with smoke and there was little talk. Behind the bar was a blonde woman in her forties, well formed and still handsome, who was serving incessantly although no one seemed to be paying.

Marya – if that was her name – led him to the empty stools at the bar. She perched on one. He, in deference to the curious males, kept standing.

'*Was möchten Sie?*' The barmaid was busily rinsing glasses as she spoke.

'*Zwei Kaffee... und zwei Whisky*,' announced Marya. At the mention of the whisky she smiled at him. He wondered if it was an oblique reference to the previous night. The waitress poured two shots of Johnny Walker.

'You like whisky?' asked Marya, noticing his expression.

'Yes, but not Johnny Walker. What you tasted last night was authentic. This stuff is made for the Americans, who don't know any better.'

'Johnny Walker is all we get here, apart from at Intershops. Maybe it is your "authentic" whisky I am after?' She smiled cheekily at him. 'What do you think?'

Their communication was becoming a tangle of Aesopian riddles, carried out in what, for both of them, was a foreign language. A game of feints, bluffs and evasions. He downed the Johnny Walker with a grimace.

'Well, if you are interested in my whisky, it is now finished. And it is not my hard currency, since I think you know that is also limited – I think you are interested in something quite different. But I don't want to know and will not ask you.'

To avoid her eyes, he looked around. What did these people think he was? An American with a good-time girl in tow?

The barmaid's eyes betrayed a flicker of interest as they met the scholar's and went hard as they surveyed the girl. He realised that people were in fact paying, for occasionally a man came to the bar and handed over money, which the barmaid took without a word. Apparently payment was based on self-accounting and trust. Except for the whisky, everything on sale here was cheap.

They finished their drinks and ascended to the cold, bare platform of Alexanderplatz station. Soon a train rattled to a halt and they entered one of its chrome and wood carriages, and swung off into the night. From the vantage point of the *S-Bahn* they could see West Berlin. The huge Axel Springer monolith was so close it appeared to be in the eastern sector itself. Its electronic news hoarding conveyed to the population of East Berlin information which their own media might have omitted to cover. She pointed this out.

'I don't know why they bother. Everyone here has Western television anyway.'

The train – and they – entered a no-man's land, walled in on either side. On both sides of the train, on both sides of the Wall, he could see washing hanging out; beyond the Wall and the wire and the searchlights, people were moving behind lighted windows. It was as if he and the girl sitting opposite were in ultimate limbo. Avoiding direct eye contact, she looked at his reflection in the window, he at hers.

'*Die Mauer*,' she said, with an incline of her head towards it.

'Two days ago it astonished me,' he said. 'Today it already seems normal.'

'People here don't notice it, don't think about it,' she stated.

'Or maybe just don't speak about it,' he said, recalling the old man in the *Ratskeller* the previous night.

'Maybe,' she conceded.

He remarked that she seemed very familiar with Berlin and asked how long she had been studying there.

'Oh, a little while. Look, it is our stop, Pankow.'

Outside the station workmen were erecting banners and posters to greet the citizens of Berlin the next day on their awakening. A huge banner hung from the railway bridge beside the station proclaiming 'Victory to the Palestinian Revolution'. Pictures of Arafat were everywhere as they walked along the dark and deserted avenue towards the *Unterbringung*. At major street junctions, the *Vopos* in their kiosks looked listlessly at their passing. Only their foot treads broke the silence.

Tonight a decision had to be made, he thought. This could still be a one-night stand, a fling paid for in a modest outlay.

The sound of their steps seemed to grow louder as they approached the door of the apartment building. In the entrance hall the odour of polished linoleum and the night scent of chrysanthemums stirred up in him memories of the tenement by the cold grey sea where he had spent his early years. Two rooms, a toilet four flights down in the back-court. But clean, spotlessly clean, and redolent of the smells of that Berlin night.

He pressed the night-light and they ascended. But on the landing below theirs

she stopped him, waited till the lights went out and held her hand over the switch to prevent him putting the light on again.

'Go home. Say there is some problem, some illness. Take your Bismarck and go home.'

He could think of nothing to say and stopped her mouth with an uncertain touch of his fingers. Then, switching on the light, they continued upstairs and entered the flat. They moved down the corridor to where their two doors faced each other. There was every reason to let her go, every reason. But they stood, uncertain, as on the previous night. He was drifting towards the rapids.

She seemed a little embarrassed now, less sure of herself as she said, 'Well, have you any more of that "authentic" whisky you gave me last night?'

'No, but I can make you a coffee if you want,' was his rather lame riposte.

In no-man's land, between the walls, the decision was taken. Her door was left unopened.

Later, as they lay together, he said, 'This was not on the agenda for my trip.'

'You are not writing the agenda,' was her reply.

Nicaragua State of Emergency

Nicaragua has declared a state of emergency, which gives the Sandinista government sweeping powers to arrest opponents and to censor the press. In the capital Managua the Nicaraguan Defence Minister stated that the U.S. was preparing an invasion of the country by anti-Sandinista forces, the "Contras", in exile in Honduras and Miami, and announced a civil defence scheme to defend the country "house by house, brick by brick". The new U.S. ambassador in Managua has denied that the U.S. is in any way organising or supporting such an invasion. He called upon the Sandinistas to hold new and free elections, stating that those which they had won recently by a landslide were flawed.

CHAPTER SEVEN

A PATTERN OF DAYS emerged. He went to the University in the morning and worked till mid-afternoon. Then he walked around the city visiting historical sights or museums relating to his research. In the evenings he met Marya. She did not come to the University very often, and was vague about her work:

'It is very boring, and I have done most of it. Only a report to write. But I don't want to finish it too quickly, or it's back to Bulgaria for me.'

What she did when he was out, he did not ask. Occasionally, in a half-mocking way, she made reference to 'your Bismarck' and asked how his work was progressing. It was going very well, he was enjoying the time spent in his eyrie at the University, in almost complete self-absorption and isolation. Only now and again did the exterior world intrude.

He was sitting in the canteen after a day's work. Behind

him he could hear an English girl talking to a group of other English students, like him, on cultural exchange – but younger. She was telling them how she had come on a day visa, hoping to get a longer-stay visa when in East Berlin – to spend some time with her boyfriend, who could wangle it through the University.

'When I got to the checkpoint, a uniformed dragon of a *Grenzpo* woman looked at my day visa and asked why I had a full suitcase. Then she told me to open it. My God, was I embarrassed! I had about a dozen packets of condoms in it. Ralph told me that the local ones were like finger stools, though how he knows, I didn't ask. Anyway, she looked at them for a while and I thought I'd be refused entry. But then she smiled and said, "*So viele Gummis für einen Tag,*" closed the case and stamped it. I felt like a proper whore after that!'

Her audience burst into laughter; public, English laughter. He decided to be up and gone before they discovered he was a compatriot. This intrusion of home had disturbed his exile, his hibernation.

At night he and Marya would meet for a meal. He discovered that with prices as they were in Berlin, a modest addition to his *Stipendium* from his equally modest supplies of foreign currency enabled him – and them – to live in style. They regularly visited the *Ermeler Haus* and the little *Shinkel Klaus*, a cameo of classic Prussian architecture used as a restaurant tucked just off the Unter den Linden.

One night she wanted home cooking and they went to a Bulgarian restaurant, the Sofia, in one of the huge apartment blocks on the Leipziger Strasse. He was surprised to find these blocks had shops and restaurants in them.

'This is like Sofia,' she noted. 'Concrete apartment blocks and nothing else. Berlin is better.'

They often went to the opera or the theatre. He found himself taken to jazz cafes where bad imitations of the kind of Western jazz he did not like were played, or to Hollywood films, which she was very enthusiastic about. He did not mind, just enjoying her company, her willingness to listen to him talking about the impressions Berlin made on him, her initiatives, which allowed him to float without responsibility.

They went to *Die Distel*, a cabaret just opposite the exit from the Friedrichstrasse station where he had first emerged into the Berlin night. The dimness of the neon lights of the Theater Metropol and dull sulphurous glow from the street lights did not cause him to peer now. They gave out enough light to see by and to walk down the alleyway to *Die Distel*, which lay behind the *Metropol*. They listened to veiled and barbed *Witze* on the *Apparatchniks* and the *Vopos*, in a racy *Berlinisch* he found hard to follow, though the general drift was obvious. At one point he asked Marya, whose German was better than his, to explain a joke that had caused great amusement.

'He said: What do you get if you cross a wolf with a *Vopo*? Answer: a very stupid wolf. That is quite good for a German joke.'

But the meaning of the singer was obvious in any language. This was Gisela May, the current queen of the Brecht chanteuses in Berlin. She had the Tarnhelm to transform herself into any shape. One minute in basque and stockings she was the vamp-whore in the '*Ballade von der sexuellen Hörigkeit*'; in seconds, wrapped in a blanket, only her face visible, Mother Courage sang of her misery.

He was without doubt leading a pleasant life, he thought as he watched the show, watched Marya. He would deal with the reckoning, when it came.

One day he told her he would be late back. He had had a phone call at Frau Hügeln's flat from the Cultural Mission to collect his mail and see about certain other matters. Frau Hügeln had fetched him and stood nearby as he talked into her phone, her arms folded. He wondered if she understood English. She had stated that she did not.

That morning after study he visited the *Märkisches Museum*, which was devoted to the history of Prussia. The building, on the banks of the Spree, was an amusing compilation of historical *Märkish* architecture, from medieval to renaissance. Outside a brown bear rolled in a deep concrete pit: it was not hibernating, he noticed, just dozing. He thought how easy it would be to tumble into, but how difficult to get out of, that pit.

He entered the museum and walked round the exhibits, making notes on the dismissive attitudes to Prussia which accompanied them. The museum was almost empty and his footfall echoed along the polished parquet floors. Echoed twice. A peculiarity of the architecture? He walked across a room, then doubled back to the entry. A man in a *Kunstleder* coat and dark glasses entered, walked past him and stared in rapt attention at a display of earthenware stoves. It was like the same bad movie again, absurd and not serious: typecast. Turning on his heels, he left the man studying the evolution of Prussian faience stoveware and went out, towards the Mission on the Unter den Linden.

At the counter he asked for his mail. The secretary handed him a couple of letters.

'I was also expecting a parcel,' he said.

'Was there a parcel for Mr...?' she leant back and shouted.

Maybe it had been stopped, maybe the invisible hand was rewriting the script.

The smiling Director emerged at the counter with a large, securely bound parcel which he held on to, lingered over, as he spoke.

'Ah, yes, no room for it out here. A parcel from home. A change of underwear or some home baking? Hope it's nothing to sell on the black market. Don't want to be getting us into trouble. We are responsible for the conduct of our Cultural Mission guests.'

He smiled, too ingratiatingly and handed over the parcel.

The recipient deposited it in his briefcase, thanked the now impassive donor and was about to leave when the Director added, 'Hold on a minute. How is, eh, Bismarck... going? Hope you're not discovering anything that could upset our friendly relations with the DDR? Now, the reason I wanted to see you was this. Your project has interested a lot of people, and the *Gesamtdeutsche Institut* in West Berlin – you know the Federal organisation dealing with,' he smiled, 'inter-German affairs would like to hear from you. You know, a little talk on your discoveries, the rehabilitation of Prussia in the DDR, that kind of thing. How about it?'

His first feeling was to refuse. He had seen the *Gesamtdeutsche Institut*'s publications; studies on the DDR by the organisation of a government which claimed to be the *de jure* ruler of all Germany. But then a thought struck him and he asked, if he did the talk, whether he could take another student with him, one he had met who was interested in his investigations.

'No problem at all, we go in CD cars. Immunity at the checkpoints and all that. As long as the student is willing to take the risk; they could get into a lot of trouble.'

Dates and times were arranged and he left. Outside, the aspiring expert on the evolution of heating systems in Prussia from the *Märkisches Museum* had become an enquirer into the customs of the British monarchy. He looked up from Charles and Diana as the scholar descended with his briefcase, then walked off in the opposite direction.

Going home in the train, the parcel unopened in his suitcase, he felt as if they were all – himself, Marya, the Mission Director – acting in a cabaret sketch. That they were still at *Die Distel*, but not in the audience this time. He looked out the window and saw a face smiling the Mitropa smile back at him: his own face.

At the flat he found she was not in his room. He knocked at her door and entered. She was visibly sulking.

'I've arranged for you to go to West Berlin,' he began, 'You are always saying how interesting it must be. The Mission Director is taking me to a meeting there, to give a talk. You can come; visit the fleshpots of the Kurfürstendamm, if you like.'

She looked up, then away again.

He continued, 'But tomorrow we will take a trip to the countryside. To the Altmark, to look for the birthplace of my hero, Otto, the Iron Chancellor.'

She looked hard at him. Finally, she spoke.

'Yes, that is a good idea. Stick to your studies. It is better, easier to study history than to try to influence it.' Her eyes moved to his briefcase. 'Did you collect your mail? Yes, I suppose you did.'

An awkwardness ensued, which he broke by suggesting that they visit the *Komisches Oper*, where *Mahagonny* was playing. She agreed, still sullen, and after a hurried meal in the *Ratskeller*, they were heading downtown in the *U-Bahn*.

'This will prepare you for the decadence of West Berlin,' he joked as they sat in the carriage. She stared out the window and did not reply. He did likewise. Again, the Wall. Again, no-man's land.

Inside the theatre, in addition to the usual tourists, Party officials and officers of the Western powers, there was a group of Tadjiks or Uzbekhs; the men sat with caps on, the women in veils. He had seen them on the Unter den Linden in the afternoon, at the 'Anti-Fascist Defense Wall'. The roulette of their theatre-ticket allocation had landed the holiday party with Brecht and Weill's portrayal of bourgeois decadence. The men sat impassive, the women with lowered eyes, as male actors drew with lipstick on women's naked breasts. Devoid of language, they saw it as voyeurism. Next to them sat a braided US officer, with a woman old enough, this time, to be his wife. She wore a clinging white crepe dress that emphasised her still very attractive body. She looked bored.

At the interval he said to Marya, 'Did you notice the Uzbekhs?'

'Yes,' she replied sharply 'But I'm surprised you did, the amount of attention you gave to that officer's whore.'

He took this as a sign that she was thawing and relaxed a little, replying, 'I think she was old enough to be his wife. Maybe she was thinking the same about you, as you thought about her?'

She smiled and took his hand as they returned to their seats.

After the interval, the Central Asian party had departed en masse. He commented to Marya that they had applied the wrong frame of reference to what they had seen. She looked at him a little condescendingly.

'Yes. As they used to tell us in Marxism-Leninism classes, dialectics is about seeing events in a proper framework.'

'You are getting serious all of a sudden,' he replied.

'You should think about that, about seeing events objectively and not from a subjective standpoint. But enough of that. Tomorrow we go hunting for the soul of old Prussia. I think the Altmark will be a bit like Bulgaria,' she said with a mock shudder.

'But we have the delights of West Berlin to come. I can assure you that will not be like Bulgaria.'

'Yes, West Berlin. You realise that you are violating border regulations by taking me there? And what if I defect?'

He watched the icy pavement passing beneath their feet. They were crossing the Spree at the Weidendammer Brucke, resplendent with cast-iron Prussian eagles.

He looked up. 'You won't,' he said.

He woke suddenly. Marya was not there. A light showed in the hall. He got up and walked along to the front door, which was open, as was that of Frau Hügeln's flat next door. Marya was on the phone and saw him standing in the doorway.

She replaced the phone and stared at him, challenging him to ask.

He obliged.

'Who were you phoning?'

'My hydraulics supervisor.'

'Do you always phone your supervisor this late at night?'

She laughed. 'It is sometimes difficult to get hold of him at normal times.'

'What did you tell him?'

'Nothing. Hydraulics, as I told you, is so boring.'

He imagined this was probably the case; but could not convince himself that it was likewise with the hydraulics expert, as she crawled into bed beside him.

Jaruzelski Berlin Welcome

General Jaruzelski, head of the government in The People's Poland, was today welcomed warmly in Berlin by members of the Central Committee of the Socialist Unity Party of Germany. In the light of the difficulties facing The People's Poland it was agreed to extend economic credits to the country beyond those previously negotiated, and also to speed up joint G.D.R.–Polish economic co-operation on projects along their mutual border. Comrade Honecker spoke for the whole Central Committee when he stated that, with fraternal help, Poland would overcome its present difficulties, learning from the past and strengthening the links between the government and the population, links which had been damaged by previous mistakes exacerbated by the meddling of international imperialism.

CHAPTER EIGHT

IN THE MORNING, the first one of March, there had been a dramatic rise in temperature. Apart from the as yet leafless trees, it seemed like summer all at once – though still sharp and fresh. Arriving at the station, they bought two tickets to Schönhausen. The booking clerk explained that they had to change at Rathenow and then catch a local train to Schönhausen. By the way he looked at them it was clear he did not sell many tickets to their destination. The scholar recalled the desk clerk at Albuquerque Greyhound bus station when he asked for a ticket to a similar New Mexican backwater, 'You wanna go to Sanna Rosa! You ever *been* to Sanna Rosa?'

Pulling out of Berlin, they passed the huge brick water towers by Storkower Strasse station. They did not stop at the station, nor at Ostkreutz, speeding past the passengers on the platform waiting for the local train. From Ostkreutz the Jews of Berlin and adjacent parts of

Germany had been taken east to the concentration camps. He mentioned this to Marya.

'I know. Sometimes I think you see me as very stupid,' she said, apparently sulking again.

'No. It's just that I'm very pedantic. It's my historical training.'

The train's noise, amplified by a tunnel, interrupted them for a moment. Then he resumed, 'For a Bulgarian hydraulics student you know a lot about Berlin.'

'*Ja, über Berlin weiss ich bescheid,*' she replied.

For a while there was only the noise of the train. Outside, forest and field, field and forest, but with the grip of winter relaxed, the brief green of crops beginning to show here and there against the sandy earth, still patched with snow. There were nests in the treetops; of storks, he supposed. In forest clearings there were lakes surrounded by weekend cottages and allotments.

Eventually the train squealed to a halt. Looking out he saw the sign: Rathenow. They descended to find the station almost deserted. A small kiosk provided them with lemonade and chocolate. Outside, the dusty town square was empty. A ten-minute walk showed them everything Rathenow had to offer. Nothing was open, as it was a Sunday, raising memories of the Presbyterian Sabbaths of his youth.

'Yes, it is just like Bulgaria!' Marya laughed.

They killed time in the station till the local train came and carried them on to Schönhausen. The journey was brief and they descended to another empty station with faded and flaking stucco walls. It was now midday, the sky clear as crystal and the heat intense. The train pulled away. They stood by the silent track.

Poplar fringed, a road led to the village about half a mile away, and along it they went. At the entry to the village, posters exhorted the reader to live and work for socialism. All the houses around the square were slumbering in the heat. The main street was cobbled and the pavements were sand.

A dog stirred sleepily in the dust, hens pecked here and there. The recurrent feeling of having erred onto a film set came again to him. Suddenly, out of nowhere, a convoy of Russian military vehicles sped past, leaving dust hanging in the air.

In the centre of the village square stood a war memorial, with a rather ungainly Prussian eagle atop. It listed the dead of Schönhausen in the Franco-Prussian War of 1871. There was no mention on the monument, which bore the date of 1895, of Bismarck, the village's most famous son. A bullet hole from 1944 or '45 neatly pocked the list of the dead, with what felt like stage-managed irony. They stood at the monument, looking around for guidance. Finally, at the far end of the street they discerned a figure working in his garden. Towards the figure they walked; the dog got up and followed them.

The scholar explained to the gardener, who continued at his labours, that he was looking for the Bismarck manor house. The man then stopped, gave a short laugh and began hoeing again. Then he stopped once more and pointed towards the red-brick *Kirche* which could be seen beyond a few more houses. And on again they went. Before the *Kirche* was an open gate leading into what appeared to be a small park. Lines of trees stood guard over sandy paths that led to a tiny lake. Youths from the village were riding scramble motorbikes round the paths.

A series of steps led down to a flattened area, where the foundations of a building were visible. The stump of a building, part of what must have been a larger house, flanked the cleared area. A helicopter passed low overhead and its updraught whirled the dead leaves around Marya and himself. For a moment, surrounded by leaves like a dryad, she was hardly visible.

She emerged laughing, with the words, 'Here is your *Geburtsort*! This is what you came for!'

The leaves slowly fell, revealing that she was right. Nothing, no memorial, just an empty space. They walked back towards the gate and asked an old man sitting on a bench about the manor house. He got quite excited, told them it had been a hospital, then a refugee centre, before it was demolished.

'We were not allowed in here before the war. The last Bismarck fled just before the Russians came.'

'Why is there no *Denkmal* to Bismarck here?'

The Mitropa smile again, and a shrug of the shoulders. As they moved away, the old man suggested, 'Go to the *Kirche*. Ask the custodian to show you round.'

They took his advice and knocked at the cottage beside the *Kirche*, the word so like the kirk he'd been forced to attend in his youth. An old lady came to the door, wiping her mouth with a napkin. The smell of food made him realise he was hungry. It was still hot and he was beginning to feel dizzy.

Before they could speak the old woman said, '*Die*

Kirche? Ja, warte fünf minuten,' and closed the door.

While they waited, they examined the *Kirche*. It was a huge building for such a small village. A fine crack split one wall from spire to ground (which the custodian later told them was a memento of the Thirty Years War, by which time the *Kirche* was already five hundred years old). By now he was feeling faint with heat and hunger and took shelter in the shadow of the church.

After a while the old woman came and opened a small wooden side-door, using a large metal key that hung from her belt. Inside, it was blissfully cool. The custodian stood at the door, arms folded, and let them wander around at will.

Everywhere were carved plaques and tombstones to the family whose private wooden pew, raised above the rest of the worshippers, was reached by a set of steps. Who used it now? A sword drawn for the Hohenzollern in every generation had been the family boast. But even here, though he had been baptised in the stone font, no mention of the Iron Chancellor, whose ashes were buried elsewhere and whose land was now a collective farm. Even a thousand years of existence had not bestowed permanence on Prussia. Their curiosity satisfied, they went out again into the blazing day. He thanked the custodian and gave her a donation for the upkeep of the church.

'Now we have had enough of dead people,' said Marya. 'Down there, through the park, is the Elbe. Let's go there and get some shelter among the trees.'

She took his hand and pulled him towards the river. They went through pine woods, by sandy paths past tiny ponds; at times he thought they were lost. But finally they emerged on the banks of the smooth, dark, swift flow of the broad Elbe.

'Another mile west and Bismarck would not have been *Ost-Elbisch*,' he mused, mind still on the past.

It was still hot, amazingly hot for early March. She turned to look at him.

'I am going to cool down in the water.'

She quickly slipped out of her clothes down to her undergarments and slid down the sandy bank to where a little backwater eddy was guarded by a fallen tree. She looked up at him.

'It is freezing, but come in. Put your stupid briefcase down and get rid of the dirt and sweat.'

He watched the water running off her as she submerged and emerged, like a naiad now, as he fantasised. With the heat and hunger he felt he was hallucinating.

Soon he was beside her and they moved carefully into the swift current, always making sure they could feel the bottom with their feet. Then she glided past him and struck out for the bank. Surprised, he moored on the fallen tree and watched as she pulled herself up the bank and began to rummage amongst his clothes. Finding the briefcase, she removed the parcel it contained and after looking at him arced it through the air and far out into the brown stream. Even had he wanted to, to retrieve it was beyond his powers. It floated before it sank, like the King of Thule's beaker. Hydraulics, the laws of water flow, were carrying it away. Briefly he felt a surge of relief. Then anger.

Shivering now, he swam slowly to the bank. She was

looking at him, half defiant, half apprehensive. In the freak, unseasonable sun the steam rose from their skins. He felt anger at the absurdity of his situation, but mainly at himself. Looking at Marya, he also felt desire increasing his anger, confirming his absurdity. She found herself the recipient of all his feelings and they coupled themselves dry, in a violence that was almost mutual rape.

Afterwards she said, 'Keep to your Junker now.'

When they returned to Berlin late that night, workmen were already festooning the city and main avenues with banners welcoming Jaruzelski to a meeting with Honecker. The picture of the general, with his dark glasses and wooden smile, was everywhere. Slogans warned of the dangers facing People's Poland from the assaults of imperialism and promised the solidarity of the DDR working class. In the *U-Bahn* going home, as he surveyed the red-bannered avenues, he felt this might be a chance to break the code in which they talked, to escape from the maze of evasions which passed as communication between them.

She did not reply for a while, after he asked, 'What do you think about what is happening in Poland? And don't say it is as boring as Bulgaria!'

The train rattled through the night towards the suburbs. Marya turned away from him and he had to look into the blackened window to see her eyes; beyond the reflection of her face were the lights, the Wall, the minefields.

'The government has made terrible mistakes in dealing with the people and the economy over the years. But the forces opposed to them are very much worse. They represent Catholic and anti-semitic Poland.'

'Yes, that is the leaders, but the workers can be beyond that, break free and fight for authentic socialism.'

She turned from the window and looked at him directly, with a hint of condescension.

'That only happens in the fantasies of romantics and in the literature they produce. Jaruzelski was necessary. If he falls, the opposition will lead Poland back to clerical domination, not to a better kind of socialism. You have to accept what is necessary, not some Utopian dream. It is funny, I am young, I should still have dreams, but you should be too old for them.'

He turned away, looked at himself in the window. Was that the choice? Jaruzelski or the Pope? At first, with the euphoria of the struggle, it had not seemed so. But was there a real alternative to the heirs of Stalin, who had led the country to ruin, or the heirs of those who had collaborated with the Holocaust and whose nationalism was vitriolic in its hatred? If not, what would the choice be? Or might there be no choice?

The rest of the journey was completed in silence until the now familiar sight of the station at Pankow was reached. They walked northwards along Mühlenstrasse, where a frost was already settling. The sky had remained clear and it would be a cold night. Stars were coming out. As they passed the *Vopo* kiosk, they noticed that its occupant was sleeping. Marya giggled.

'The ever-vigilant defense forces of the proletariat at work.'

He smiled at the sight of the podgy, sleeping policeman,

but then said pointedly, 'Someone followed me to the Mission when I went to collect that parcel you disposed of.'

She looked at him in apparent surprise. Then hissed between her teeth, 'And you think that I have informed on you? That maybe I have been appointed to watch you? That I am some kind of Mata Hari? You have a very high opinion of your importance!'

He was about to apologise, to continue the lie, but she walked on ahead, quickly.

He listened to the sound of her heels on the pavement. He had always loved the sound of a woman walking in high-heels, though his enjoyment seemed perverse at that moment.

She did not answer when he knocked at her door.

After a moment he asked, through the door, 'How did you know? About the parcel and what was in it?' He saw her figure through the frosted glass. He could see her outline and he wanted to be beside it. 'How did you know that they were leaflets about Poland?'

'You talk in your sleep.'

He felt like asking, 'In German?' but did not.

'And then though you have a lock in your briefcase, you have no key. Some agitator. Out of curiosity, I looked.'

Before he could ask anything else, the doorknob clicked back.

'Come in. Maybe I can learn some more secrets of high espionage tonight.'

'So why...' he began.

'Stupid. I just did not want you to do anything silly.

We are enjoying Berlin together, I think? So, why spoil that for something pointless?'

He knew she was lying. But he was prepared to accept the lie, relinquish responsibility for his own fate to this woman, this girl whose will seemed so much stronger than his. His priorities were altering; she was becoming more important to him than his original reasons for being in Berlin. Though we cannot jump over our shadows, he thought, we can take shelter in the shadows cast by others. He would – for a while – shelter in hers.

Soviets Battling Mujihadeen in Helmand

Heavy fighting in Helmand province between Soviet forces and their Afghan allies and the Mujihadeen guerrillas appears to have resulted in the Red Army withdrawing from the remoter areas to more secure bases. From the areas taken by the guerrillas, disturbing reports are emanating of reprisals, including the public rape and stoning to death of female schoolteachers and the flaying alive of captured Soviet soldiers, but any such reports are difficult to verify. Babrak Karmal, General Secretary of the People's Democratic Party of Afghanistan, stressed that the fight of the Afghan people with the support of their Soviet allies against the forces of clericalism and feudalism would go on till victory.

CHAPTER NINE

THE BRIEF, UNSEASONAL warm spell did not last. It reverted to winter, the intense winter of Central Europe. The snow, which had melted, turned to ice. The climate agreed with him: the crisp, dry days slowly became less cold. Better than the slush and fog of home, he thought. The familiar pattern of days continued.

Soon it was the occasion of his talk in West Berlin, for which he had prepared half-heartedly although his researches had gone well. He would be able to carry it out. He organised some papers together in a folder and began composing his thoughts as he dressed. Then he and Marya took the *U-Bahn* to the Cultural Mission, where they waited in the foyer for the Director. Marya flicked through the Western magazines and colour supplements while they waited. The Director appeared, halted when he saw Marya, and raised a diplomatic eyebrow.

'Well, well, I didn't realise… International relations,

eh? Well, well. I hope you've impressed on the young lady the importance of discretion. We don't want any diplomatic complications, do we?'

They entered a car which was waiting outside, the Director and driver in front, he and Marya in the rear. They moved off smoothly towards the border.

'What kind of car is this?' asked Marya admiringly.

'I don't know. A Daimler, I think,' the scholar replied in bad humour at her question.

'Yes, it's a Daimler, all right. Can't afford Rolls-Royces in these days of imperial decline. And it would look a trifle out of place in the workers' state,' added the Director, with what he intended as an impish grin. The scholar noticed that the Director appeared very pleased with himself and was in an excellent mood.

'Lenin had a Rolls-Royce,' the scholar corrected. 'A yellow one.'

'Oh, did he?' was the drawled reply.

By now they had arrived at *Grenzübergang Friedrichstrasse*, known beyond as Checkpoint Charlie. They entered the diplomatic lane, where there were no formalities, though a camera recorded their passing, and crossed the stripe in the road that marked the frontier between the two Berlins: the two worlds. Marya, he noted, was attentive, on the edge of her seat.

At first they encountered a mirror-image of the territory bordering the Wall on the East; cleared spaces, ruined buildings. But on the Western side the Wall was painted with slogans and graffiti. They then moved through Kreutzberg, an area of tenements filled with Turkish *Gastarbeiter* and daubed with the slogans of the *alternativ* Berlin leftists. Take away the slogans and the Turks and it could have been the Penzlauer Berg in the East, the scholar thought. They passed a ruined facade with a tree growing out of it, facing a vacant lot where a market was in progress.

'That's the *Anhalter Bahnhof*, or was,' said the Director, 'We'll be at the *Gesamtdeutsche Institut* soon.'

Soon they were in bourgeois Berlin: wide avenues crowded with BMWs and Mercedes, pavements trodden by well-dressed women, streets lined with de-luxe shops. He could see that Marya was mesmerised by what she saw.

On his home ground, more confident now, he said, 'City centres in the West are for the bourgeoisie. They are visible, the poverty is not. Shops are full of luxuries but not everyone can buy.'

Marya seemed to be so engrossed by what she was seeing that he felt she had hardly heard him.

He carried on, 'You know the lines from *Dreigroschenoper*: ' *Man sieht die im Lichte, die im Dunkeln sieht man nicht*'? That is the West.'

Again, she did not reply.

The car came to a halt and they were ushered into a building whose windows displayed pamphlets on 'The German Question'. Inside an audience of around forty academics and government officials awaited their arrival in a small hall. The chairman, immaculate in the businessman's suit that West German academics seemed to favour, introduced him benignly as a 'very learned scholar'. Members of the audience rapped their knuckles on the tables in appreciation.

He took the floor. By now, his German was equal to the task of presenting his thesis.

After a period of rejection of all things Prussian as products of militarism and aggression, the DDR historical community was now giving credit to the progressive elements in Prussian history, in order to help forge a national identity. Just as Marx and Engels had analysed it, the Prussian-led unification was now seen as progressive by DDR writers. The former idea that a popular revolution could have unified Germany was being abandoned, as was any idea that Germany could ever be reunited.

The audience listened politely, apart from one man who was taking notes so fast, they had to be in shorthand. And Marya, who was looking at him with quizzical fixity. When he had finished the chairman thanked him for his 'learned contribution', the audience repeated the ritual of knuckle-rapping and the chairman asked for questions. The scholar had an idea what was coming.

'What problems have you had with the DDR academic authorities in your research?' was the first enquiry.

'None. They seem totally uninterested in me and have left me alone ever since I arrived. I think they have forgotten I am there. Though doubtless there are others who are keeping an eye on me.'

'Do you think that this is because your subject is one upon which they are unwilling to comment, because of its sensitive nature?'

'Possibly.'

'What is your opinion of academics in the DDR?'

'They work harder, but earn less, than those in the West.'

Polite laughter greeted this response. Marya was smiling. The shorthand writer wrote on.

'What problems have you come across, living in the East?'

'None, really.'

'But surely you must have encountered some difficulties?'

He paused for a moment, annoyed that none of the questions were about his actual research, though he had expected this.

'My room is a trifle over-heated but if you open the window it is all right. And I have found that the supply of pineapples can be a bit erratic.'

A silence ensued. The chairman brought the meeting to a close, again thanking his 'learned colleague'. There was more knuckle-rattling on tables and exchanges of handshakes. As the scholar stepped down from the podium, the Director approached him.

'I say, we did ruffle a few feathers there. I do believe you'll be defecting if you stay behind the Wall much longer. Clearly life agrees with you there.'

And he gave what was intended to be a man-of-the-world smile towards Marya, who was approaching.

'If they ask stupid questions about the DDR, instead of about my work, they can't be offended by the answers they get.'

Marya had now arrived at his side, smiling. 'I did not know you had a sense of humour. I thought the British were humourless, just like the Germans,' she observed.

'My friend would like to see West Berlin,' he informed the Director. 'Is it possible that we could return later?'

The diplomat seemed delighted to oblige.

'No problem at all. Where would you like to be picked up? I'll send a car.'

'*Anhalter Bahnhof*, at eleven o'clock?'

Assuring them that all would be well with the arrangements, the Director headed back East, leaving them, like a couple of truants, on the pavement.

'First, let's eat. But I'm afraid, this side of the Wall, it will have to be a pizzeria.'

She loved it; the informality, the speed of service, the – to her – exoticism of the Italian waiters.

'They teach them that accent, along with the cooking,' he grouched.

The glitter of the city dazzled her; they spent a couple of hours in the Ka De We department store, where she bought shoes, stockings, cosmetics.

'This is cheaper than on the other side,' she justified herself. She had no hard currency; he paid. It was pleasant to pretend that he was paying for his pleasures. He also did not tell her that Ka De We was only middle-market shopping. As they strolled along the Ku'Damm, Marya seemed to take an almost sensual delight in window-shopping. He realised that for her this must be what he had experienced when he first went East: disorientation, fascination. But he was getting bored with all this consumerist voyeurism and when he saw a bus approaching, its sign announcing it was going to the Olympic Stadium, he seized her hand and along with it the chance to regain control and announced, 'Come on, let's do a little sightseeing.'

'You have been very decisive since you came back to the

West,' she teased as they boarded and paid the driver.

'It is easier to be decisive here. Things are clearer and there are no consequences.'

The bus drove through the island of free enterprise, with its Federal-subsidised affluence. Marya, as he now knew, was loyal to the system on the other side; but she was clearly bowled over by the visible wealth.

'There is nowhere like this in Bulgaria!' she laughed.

'There is nowhere like this in Scotland,' he responded. 'Where I live, a third of all men are out of work.'

He noticed she was not paying a great deal of attention to what he said. They descended at a dusty, tree-lined space. They could see the stadium at the far end, with the Olympic Bell Tower. As they entered, they realised to their mutual surprise that Hitler's stadium for the 1936 Games was not a ruin. It was used by the local West Berlin football team. The Olympic pool was full of swimmers.

As they walked around the empty stadium under the gaze of its massive Aryan figures, they looked in vain for some mention of Hitler, to whose master race this was to be one of the monuments.

'Nothing about the Thousand Year Reich or Nazism,' Marya commented, adding, 'I think this should have been razed to the ground.'

'History upsets people here. They want to forget it, say it's ended, over.'

They walked away from the silent, menacing place.

On the bus on way back to the centre of the city, she asked, 'Why did you want to go there?'

'To give you something more that Ka De We to remember West Berlin by.'

It was dusk and the lights of cinemas, restaurants and night clubs were coming on. The beggars were soliciting small change from the well-heeled pleasure seekers and at street corners there were groups of prostitutes in short skirts and plunging necklines. Marya gaped at the whole scene, stunned by the riot of noise, light and people.

A shower of rain started. For shelter they entered a bar, quaintly called Bovril. He thought that possibly it sounded romantic in German. The decor was art deco, the clientele designer-clad. Behind the bar was a stunning blonde in a red dress. Marya watched him closely as he gave the barmaid their order.

'For an idealist, you are easily interested in a pair of nice legs.'

'You agree they were nice? Anyway, you seemed to be very taken by the delights of the commodity economy this afternoon.'

The silence that ensued lasted until they had finished eating. Then he said, 'There used to be a saying – it came from France in '68. "Capitalism is a carnivorous flower". I thought it was just a nice turn of phrase, now I'm beginning to know what it means. Especially here, in a place like West Berlin.'

'You were one of the ultra leftist petty bourgeois students of that period?'

He hesitated a little, trying to compose his mind and feelings about that epoch, when to be a realist was to demand the impossible. Grosvenor Square when the US Embassy was attacked, Paris when the barricades were up, Derry when the guns came out: had it all really happened? It seemed like another lifetime.

'That period saw the re-birth in the West of the idea that human beings could end exploitation, triumph over evil. And certainly I shared the illusions of the epoch. But for a long time, I have been shedding those illusions…'

'You don't atone for lost illusions by ridiculous gestures that lead nowhere but to punishment. That is like some Christian doctrine of suffering and redemption. You have to look at what is objectively possible and support a system that establishes a minimum of human justice…'

'You are talking again like a Stalinist party manual,' he snapped angrily. 'Is a system where only foreigners and Party hacks are allowed into luxury hard-currency shops based on justice?'

'Here, everyone can go into Ka De We but not everyone can buy. That is democracy.'

'So? You are not going to defect? You think the East is better after all? In that case, let us go back.'

Surrounded by the noise of the Berlin night, they walked back to the unfashionable district around the *Anhalter Bahnhof* ruins and waited for the Daimler. Midnight came, but the Daimler did not. They watched for it from a bar opposite the ruins; around them, Turks drank and gambled.

'That shit of a Director has done this on purpose,' Marya suggested.

'Why would he do that?'

'He probably has his reasons,' she replied.

'What can we do? We cannot go to the border. You have no exit visa, they would arrest you.'

'Tomorrow,' said Marya unconcernedly, 'we can go back in a tourist bus. They never check them for "border violations" going in, only coming out.'

'But what about tonight,' he fretted.

She was still enjoying finding herself the centre of attraction with the Turks. And she was drinking: steadily, furiously.

'We can get a room in a hotel, there are plenty here,' and she gestured vaguely out of the window at the various neon signs advertising accommodation, adding, 'You have money.'

'But these look like hotels for prostitutes and their customers,' he objected.

She looked at him lingeringly: she was very drunk now. And then she rose and went to the toilet. When she came back she was wearing some of her day's purchases. She had changed into a short skirt, donned a lace top and high-heels, and had made up her face so that she presented a passable imitation of the streetwalkers she had seen. The Turks looked bemused, he looked away, embarrassed – then back – as she tottered a little unsteadily towards him.

'I think you must find me very dowdy compared with all these Western women. Well, will I do now? Do you think they will give us a room? Am I decadent enough for my one night in the West?'

Despite his embarrassment, he felt a strong stirring of excitement. This woman, this young girl, had the capacity to totally disorient him, free him of restraint, make him feel under alien control. Absolve him of all guilt, all responsibility. Taking her arm, he hurried her out of the bar.

At the desk, a receptionist in a soiled shirt, smelling

sourly of drink, only asked, '*Eine Stunde oder eine Nacht?*'

He claimed the night and paid his dues. Thoughts of recrossing the Wall, of what lay ahead, were far from his mind as he became the willing accessory to another's fantasy of degradation. He did not understand. He did not want to understand, he had had enough of trying to understand.

UK Jobless Total Hits 3 Million

For the first time since the 1930s the number of registered unemployed in the United Kingdom has topped the three million mark, though most observers agree that the real total of unemployed, including those not eligible for unemployment benefit, is nearer to 4 million. The Employment Minister, Norman Tebbit, blamed the steep rise last month on the very cold weather, but Mrs Thatcher is coming under increasing pressure both from the "wets" in her Cabinet and from the Confederation of British Industry to modify her hard-line economic policies, which are seen by critics as leading to the destruction of the British manufacturing industry. In the wake of the news, the London Stock Market recorded one of its largest falls in over 50 years.

CHAPTER TEN

IN THE MORNING they walked to the *Gedächtniskirche*, a bombed and still ruined relic of Imperial Germany and investigated the day trips to East Berlin offered by tourist bus companies. For these, no entry or exit visa was necessary. Checks on entry were perfunctory, a little less so on exit, in case of any 'border violation', the DDR euphemism for refugee attempts. They chose a museums tour which was patronised almost exclusively by cheerful, camera-toting Americans.

At the *Grenzübergang*, the bus was boarded by a *Grenzpolizist*, who counted the passengers, then moved down the aisle randomly checking passports. He stopped at their seat.

'Pass,' he commanded.

The scholar removed his passport from his pocket; he had a long-term visa for the DDR capital, but no exit visa to West Berlin. This would be obvious if the border guard checked the document he held out. Marya pretended to be dozing.

The *Grenzpolizist* looked at the blue cover and waved it away, 'Ah, *Grossbritannien*, OK,' and passed on.

He was only interested in those with West German passports, which could be used by attempting defectors. The scholar returned the passport to his pocket. Marya opened her eyes and winked at him. She was clearly finding it great fun. It occurred to him that she knew she was in no danger.

The bus glided the short distance along the Unter den Linden, whose attractions were described by the bilingual *Berolina* guide, and stopped outside the Pergamon Museum. Marya was all for slipping off, but his caution prevailed.

'We'll follow the party in, then disappear.'

'You have the makings of a master-spy,' she teased.

They ascended the steps of the museum with the throng. He found himself listening to the guide's account of the Babylonian and Assyrian exhibits. Turning a corner, he was stunned to see the Ishtar gate of Babylon, in lapis lazuli, directly before them. Even the Americans gasped and fell momentarily silent. Marya was becoming impatient.

'Listen, the crowd is moving on, let us go.'

Outside as they crossed the Marx-Engels Brücke, he said, 'I want to go and see the Director about why no car came. I'll meet you back at the apartment.'

Marya frowned.

'I don't like him. Don't trust him.'

'You are just unfamiliar with the inefficiency of our

ruling classes. It is an endearing national characteristic.'

At the Cultural Mission things seemed to be in something of a turmoil and he had to wait some time before the Director entered.

'Oh, good God! Our Bismarck doctor!' he exclaimed, struck with sudden remembrance. ' I forgot all about you. We had a bit of a stushie here last night.' He lowered his voice to a stage whisper, 'We had a security alert. The telex has been buzzing all day. We suspect a DDR bugging attempt but the local police are taking the line that it was all a mistake, burglars at the back of the Mission, mistaking us for the Intershop next door! My humblest apologies for not having you picked up. How did you get back? You should have rung from West Berlin and I'd have sent a car.'

The Director listened to the scholar's tale with mock admiration.

'My, my, that was a nice ruse. I think we should see about recruiting you for counter-espionage. You seem to have talent.' The scholar rose to leave, but the Director continued, 'By the way, there's some more mail for you; – another parcel. What are you up to? Selling jeans on the black market to increase your *Stipendium*?' Turning to reception he called, 'Bring the doctor's mail, please,' – before continuing, 'We're having a little do here this evening, at 8. Garden party without the garden. Cultural exchange with the locals. Deadly dull, one of the burdens of office. I'd like you to come, maybe bring your… friend as well. I'll send a car. This time it will arrive.'

The secretary of the manicured nails now brought his mail, a parcel he immediately recognised as coming from the same source as the first. He took it and left. Again he faced the choice he thought Marya's grand gesture on the banks of the Elbe had deprived him of.

To keep an option open for himself, he decided to conceal the arrival of the second parcel more successfully than he had the first. Before returning to the *Unterbringung*, he visited the *Gepäckannahme* at Friedrichstrasse and received an innocuous ticket in return for the packet.

When he returned to the flat, he found that they had company. In the kitchen, drinking tea with Marya, was a Russian student.

'Ivan,' the latter beamed, holding out a firm hand in greeting. He was like an American, open and ingenuous. He also had the clean-cut, good-looking demeanour of American youth. Marya appeared to be quite intrigued by him. Kindred Slavic souls, the scholar thought.

Ivan was from Moscow, but sang the praises of Leningrad. 'Ah, the White Nights... and history! That is the place for you to go, for history.' Then he looked puzzled, like a child and asked, 'Tell me, today I am in the Unter den Linden. And I see a jeep full of American soldiers, with guns, and they are driving around. I think there is a war! What is happening?'

The scholar's erudition displaced Ivan from centre stage, as he explained the post-war agreement between the Four Powers, allowing bilateral patrols in both parts of the city.

'You would see, if you could go there, Soviet patrols in West Berlin also.'

The puzzled furrows that lined Ivan's brow disappeared.

'Let us all go out to eat,' he suggested. 'And then to a club or a cafe?'

He looked at the scholar and Marya in turn. This was the Russian's opening gambit. Ivan could not be aware of the relationship that already existed in the flat. And besides, the scholar thought, what claim did he have on the girl? He waited for her answer. 'Yes, let us go to the *Ratskeller* and then to the *Kulturclub*; there is a jazz concert tonight.'

The scholar found himself annoyed, and annoyed at his annoyance.

'I have to go to a reception at the Cultural Mission tonight. You two go, enjoy yourselves.'

He forced a smile and went to his room. Waiting for the Mission car he drank *Branntwein*. The Talisker was finished. He heard Marya and Ivan go out. Shortly afterwards, the car came for him.

In the foyer of the Mission, formally dressed British officials and their ddr counterparts mingled with token academics in tweed and intellectuals in jeans. The Mission officials conversed in bad German with their guests and made comments sotto voce in English, in the assumption that the locals could not speak the language. The purpose of the gathering was unclear. Knots of people stood about, happy to drink the gratis alcohol. After his usual snide comments, the Director left the scholar to talk to locals in imitations of the inane conversations he had had twenty years ago with foreigners in British youth hostels, on topics such as the weather and currency exchange rates.

A small jazz band was playing and a few people started dancing. He was enjoying being morbid and drowning the morbidity in alcohol but was thinking how soon he could politely leave when he saw the secretary of the manicured nails detach herself from a group of awkwardly smiling Germans and stagger a little uneasily towards the table, towards the drinks, towards himself. At the table, reaching for a glass, she bumped into him.

'Sorry,' she apologised, 'but now we have been introduced, give me a dance.' And she led him without ceremony into the midst of the dancers, where he made clumsy movements, till she gripped him close to her and led him around the floor.

Quietly, in a mildly amused tone, she whispered, 'They're on to you. They know what you're up to.'

He said nothing.

'Don't pretend you don't know what I am talking about. Your precious parcels.'

'Why are you telling me this?'

'I have my reasons.' Then, flippantly, 'Reasons of the heart. You know, *Hell hath no fury…* Bet you didn't think I knew Shakespeare?' she added aggressively, suddenly quitting the dance floor, leaving him standing alone.

After shaking many hands, he collected his coat and left.

He was the first to arrive back at the flat. He sat up, waiting for the others to return. It was after midnight when the front door opened and he heard sounds of high spirits in a language he did not understand. The voices then continued in hushed whispers; a discussion was taking place. He heard a door open and close. He held his breath as memories of his first night there came back.

Then another door opened and closed, and he breathed in relief, instantly subsumed by self-disgust at his jealousy – what claims did he have on Marya, he who was leaving in a few weeks?

The glass on his door was tapped and she came in uninvited, but stood uncertainly by the door. He felt unresponsive and managed woodenly, 'Did you have a nice time? Was the jazz concert enjoyable?'

'Why did you not come? You did not need to go to that stupid reception. Or you could have asked me to come with you.'

'I thought maybe you would rather go out with Ivan and I might be in the way. He is clearly attracted to you. I thought maybe you wanted us to compete for you. But I never fight over women, it's old-fashioned.'

She came closer.

'Well, it's clear you don't fight them off either, because you smell like you've been in a brothel.'

She gave him a piercing look, breathing audibly.

'There was dancing at the reception,' he said lamely. 'And anyway, I didn't think they had brothels in the workers' paradise of Bulgaria, so how would you know?'

'You don't fight for women, because you can never make up your mind about women, or anything else. But no, I think you *have* made up your mind. You are going home and you want to pass me on to someone else.'

He went to her and held her, but she was rigid.

'What can I do? I am going home before too long, as you say.'

'But what do you think of me? Do you feel nothing?

Was I just something to keep you warm while you wrote silly articles and had fantasies about influencing history?'

'You don't think much of me, it seems.'

'Again, you avoid the question. If you feel something, you must act. Where is your passion? Do you have water in the veins in your country?'

'I didn't start the relationship...'

'Don't avoid the issue,' she interrupted, almost shouting, 'Answer!'

She was right, of course, right in everything. He had acted very shabbily all along, refusing to face the consequences of his cosy situation; and now he owed her... himself... an answer.

'I cannot stay here. You cannot go West.'

'That is not the point! What do you feel? And then the other questions!'

Silence, take refuge in silence. But this time neither she, nor his guilt would allow silence. And to be silent would be to lose her.

'You fascinate me, obsess me. But I think the fascination we – I – feel comes from the situation we are in, which is... unusual. In cold grey Scotland or boring Bulgaria, it would be different, I think.'

'You spend your life thinking of reasons for inaction.'

Postpone a crisis and hope everything sorts itself out, he thought, offering:

'I'll apply for an extension to my stay.'

'What a lover, passion on credit!' she spat.

'I'll apply for an exchange here – maybe for a year – and we'll see how things work out.'

'So, passion with an insurance policy!'

'OK, I'll defect. Will that suit you?'

'It would be very easy for you to get a job here, they are desperate for people who can teach in English...' she began what sounded like a prepared speech.

He interrupted.

'I don't want to lose you. I'll see if it's possible to stay here.'

She unstiffened. He would think about what he had promised later. Now he was wiping out one stain, with another.

Jaruzelski in Moscow Summit on Poland

General Jaruzelski is in Moscow for talks with the Soviet Politburo about the situation in Poland. Prior to the meeting a message on Soviet radio and television emanating from the Politburo stated that "We expect the Polish Communist party leadership to continue its determined and radical steps to end the malicious anti-Soviet and anti-Communist activities of the Solidarity movement." At the same time a Soviet military spokesman stated that the current Warsaw Pact manoeuvres on the Polish–D.R.R. border had been scheduled long ago and had nothing to do with internal events in Poland.

CHAPTER ELEVEN

HE MET FRAU HÜGELN on the landing as he was leaving the flat next morning. She was smiling to herself and holding up a broken sweeping brush.

'*Ich habe zu viel gearbeitet,*' she laughed.

He thought again that Frau Hügeln was not the stuff of which socialist heroines of labour were made, not one to over-fulfill her work-norms. Her cleaning of his room had become quite perfunctory; not that he was bothered. She detained him with a question as he moved off.

'*Sie waren in West Berlin?*'

He wondered how she knew but agreed that he had been there. When she then asked which he had liked best, East or West Berlin, and he made a noncommittal response, she eyed him keenly, before saying, '*Dort haben sie mehr Geld, aber hier ist das Leben gemütlicher.*'

'*Vielleicht,*' he smiled back and at once realised that he was giving the ambiguous Mitropa smile which was here used to convey and cover meaning.

He descended the stairs thinking; yes, for him here life was certainly pleasant. He had freedom from normal restraints, freedom from the demands of work. But he could not stay here, even for a year or so; he had lied to Marya. He thought of the packet in the left luggage at Friedrichstrasse which gave him the means to avoid one choice by making another.

For a change, he walked in the fresh spring morning, through Pankow Schlosspark, where pensioners were feeding the ducks, and then on to the Heinersdorf *S-Bahn* station. Outside the local primary school children were playing in a sandpit, in the sunshine. The walls of the school were adorned with socialist-realist folk art depicting children of the world at peace and at play. On such a morning, one could almost believe it. The train swept him through town to the increasingly familiar Friedrichstrasse station. The rather casual interest taking in him by the *Sektion Geschichte* had resulted in a note on his desk one morning, from Dr Feld, asking him to give a talk on his researches to the Advanced Historical Seminar. As he entered her office, she cocked her head at him.

'Ah, the Scottish scholar. Come, the *Sektion* awaits!'

She led him along a corridor to a room, sparely furnished and with the usual picture of Honecker attempting a constipated smile behind the dais. She told him most of the small audience were historians from the University, and a couple of members of the Academy of Science. More hand-shaking.

He gave his talk about German unification, territorial traditions and the revolution in DDR historiography.

The chairman thanked him, adding that this was the first he himself had heard about a revolution in DDR historiography. From the audience came questions.

'You think our method had been un-Marxist?'

'Yes, though now it is moving closer to what Marx and Engels said. But providing the DDR with historical legitimacy is also one of the motives behind this historiographical revolution.'

'But do you not agree that after the war, when Prussianism was identified with Hitlerism, it was necessary to uproot these ideas from the people?'

'Yes, possibly. But now you have to admit what is realistic; and only Bismarckism was realistic a hundred years ago.'

As he surveyed the audience, he was suddenly jolted by seeing the same man – or so he thought – who had scribbled so much and said nothing at the *Gesamtdeutsche Institut*. This time though, he did speak.

'You say we must be realistic. To look at what is historically possible, not desirable. But we also have to define our positions to today's struggles. What is the point of these researches in the DDR; are they to be used in favour of it, or against it?'

Murmurings and sharp looks from the audience protested against this rough wooing of the speaker.

'What people make – if they make anything – of my researches will be in the light of what they already think,' he replied. 'Supporters of the DDR will say it is an overdue correction allowing the state to sink roots in the past, opponents will say it proves the origins of the DDR lie in undemocractic traditions.'

After the rituals of chairman's thanks and rapping knuckles, the meeting broke up.

At the door, Dr Feld apologised to him. 'We still have some people who are a little Stalinist in their methods.'

'It was a valid question. I do not object to it being asked.'

She smiled at him, then led him downstairs towards the canteen, where they sat drinking coffee.

'What will you do now? It sounds as if your research is almost finished.'

'I think I will make a journey to some of the other parts of the DDR and see a little more of Berlin and its surroundings.'

She seemed to approve of this and plied him with advice about where to visit: Potsdam, Rostock, Weimar. She enquired about his accommodation.

'You were only supposed to be there a couple of days but we forgot about you. We usually keep all the foreigners from the *kapitalistisches Ausland* together in one place, at a hotel or something...'

'To keep an eye on them?' he suggested.

'No, usually they prefer it, because of the foreign currency shops. Pankow is a bit of a backwater, but you are happy to remain there?'

'Yes, I have everything I want, it makes me feel less of a tourist.'

'What of the other students? Do you make contacts?'

'Oh, they come and go. It is interesting to talk.'

'So, *alles ist gemütlich?*' and she rose to go, offering her hand. 'We will meet when you return from your *Rundfahrt*, I hope? There is one problem though, your visa is only for Berlin. But things here are not so inflexible as you might think. I will write you letters of introduction to colleagues in the places you want to visit; take these to the *Grenzpolizei* offices in the Stadtmitte, and they will give you a countrywide DDR visa. The letters will be waiting for you at *Sektion Geschichte* tomorrow.'

He thanked her for this service and was wondering whether everything would stay quite so *gemütlich*, when, uninvited, someone whom he had seen at his talk sat down beside him. His accent revealed him as an American.

'Don't mind me sitting here? I just wanted to say that was a rousing talk, better than the usual wooden clichés we get here. You could see how bemused they all were by what you said, though they'd all be repeating it tomorrow if it was said in *Neues Deutschland* today. Let me introduce myself. I'm a freelance journalist working here in the DDR and I was thinking I might write something for *Junge Welt*, the FDJ magazine, about what you have been saying.'

'A freelance journalist?' the scholar interrupted. 'In the DDR? Do they exist? And American? Pardon my astonishment.'

'It's a long story. I defected during the Vietnam War and I've been here ever since. Yeah, I'm freelance, I get a lot of work about Western issues and I get away with murder compared to other journalists, don't ask me why. Maybe because I'm not a Party hack – I'm not even in the SED – so they think I have more credibility. With them there is a dialectical problem with the population.'

'Which is…'

'When they tell lies nobody believes them, but when

they tell the truth nobody believes them either. I've got a commission just now for *Schwartze Kanal* – you don't know it? It's the only DDR TV programme people watch. It combats the propaganda put out in the West about the country. It is being said the Jewish synagogue – at the *Oranienburger Tor* – is left in ruins because of anti-semitism here. If Honecker says that's not true people will think it's certain; if I – a Jewish American – say it's not true, they might just believe me. So I suppose I am quite useful. There are plenty of work opportunities for foreign defectors here and they don't keep them on a very short lead, either, they're so keen to have any at all.'

'Do you like living here?'

'The bonehead bureaucrats and the shortages are a pain in the ass, but it has its compensations, as I'm sure you've discovered already. Anyway, my phone number is on this piece of paper. Give me a call if you want to be interviewed.'

He watched the American leave and dropped the calling card in a litter basket as he headed for the station.

He met Ivan in the kitchen and received a rueful smile and an offer to share his Russian tea. He took the proffered cup.

'I have no luck with the women,' sighed Ivan, 'I get so far, and then...'

He tailed off, opened his arms expansively and then let them drop by his side.

'Maybe you are too direct,' the scholar suggested, sipping the tea. 'Try to be a bit more mysterious. Women like that.'

'Too direct? Mysterious?' Ivan considered seriously. 'But that is a little dishonest, is it not? What about socialist morality?' And then he smiled. 'Ah, but coming from a capitalist country, you will not know about socialist morality.'

The scholar had to admit that this was the case. At that point Marya came in, again behaving as if she had no special relationship with either of them.

Ivan looked at her with soulful Slavic intensity and asked, 'Would you like to go to the cinema tonight? They are showing *The Towering Inferno.*'

She pleasantly declined his offer. Ivan, now mercurially cheerful, made his exit.

Once he was gone Marya said, 'Actually, I would like to go to the cinema tonight, to see *The Last Waltz*. Bob Dylan is a very progressive artist,' she concluded with mock pomposity.

A little surprised at the cultural fare offered to the DDR citizens, he agreed and told her, 'In a few days I will be going on a trip, for historical and cultural purposes, to some of the provincial centres in the DDR. Would you like to come with me?'

'That would be fun,' she replied. 'And what about your defection?'

'I have applied for an extension of my stay with the Cultural Mission. On our return we will contact the Ministry of Education, about the possibility of work here for me,' he lied.

'Fine,' she said, 'let us go to eat, and then to the *Kino.*' He could not believe that she believed him.

The *Kino* lay off the Rosa Luxemburg Platz,

surrounded by a maze of working-class tenements behind the overhead railway line near the city centre. Here the Nazis had besieged the KPD headquarters in 1933 and with the aid of the police had gained control of the streets of Berlin – a city where they had little support. Following the *Machtergreifung*, the city had been plastered with *Berlin bleibt rot!* slogans – until the murder of those painting them. Inside the *Kino* a plaque commemorated two cinema workers killed by the Nazis. The furnishings were bare – linoleum flooring and unpadded seats. It was full of casually dressed young people. For this film there was a special surcharge, raising the total price, he calculated, by forty pence.

He told Marya, 'I saw this film when it was made. It is quite old. And Dylan is no longer radical. He took to Jesus a while ago.'

'You Westerners are so sophisticated,' she mocked, 'and you too are quite old and not as radical as you once were.'

He looked around at the audience, feeling a little awkward at the fact that he was most mature there by a decade or more. The lights went down and the film started. He found himself following the German subtitles rather than the English dialogue, except for the songs. And here again the sense of stage-managed irony intruded, the lyrics making him smile weakly at the idea of staying 'Forever Young'.

Outside after the film, in the dark they crossed the square and walked along Wilhelm Pieck Strasse, to a small *Kneipe* full of working men and women, drinking noisily at tables covered in red-and-white checked wax cloth. At every order the waitress added a stroke, or strokes, to a beer mat on the customer's table and on leaving, the drinker presented the mat at the counter and paid accordingly. He remembered being told before he came, 'Only in the East do the real *Kneipe* survive.' He saw himself over a quarter century before – waiting outside a pub like this for his father, looking in every time the door opened, to the smoke and the brightness, to the cloth-capped men.

'*Sie sind aus dem Westen?*' asked the barman.

He said that he was, but Marya was not.

'*Ah, so,*' said the barman, digesting this point. '*Und Sie finden das Leben hier angenehm?*'

Once again, he was forced to agree that life, at the moment, was indeed pleasant.

'My sister, she left the DDR. She lives in Manchester. She has a nice house. We have seen pictures, but I have not been there, of course,' the barman added, wiping glasses and placing them on shelves. 'She has a nice car too. Here we have to wait ten years for a new car…'

'Did your sister write to you about the riots in Moss Side last year? When unemployed kids threw petrol bombs at the police who baton-charged them?'

'Riots? No, she did not say.'

'Maybe she didn't notice,' the scholar suggested.

'I would like to go there and see her.'

'The climate is very bad. It rains all the time.'

'Where are you from?'

'Scotland. It rains there all the time as well. But we have no riots. We think too much. Such men are not dangerous.'

They chatted on. Occasionally another customer would come over to hear the talk, or to make a contribution. All wanted to know what he thought about the DDR and what he was doing there. They were bought drinks and he was plied with questions about the West; to his audience it was a land of milk and honey, the image gained from West German TV and American films. It did not seem to matter that there was unemployment and homelessness: not that they disbelieved, it just didn't matter. You could get a car there on credit, a good one. He could not handle the arguments. He did not want to defend the DDR, but neither did he want to defend the West. He was checkmated by these people's fascination with forbidden fruits. By their naivety, similar to that of Americans he had spoken to, bred of a different kind of isolation, an isolation enforced by the Wall.

When it was discovered that Marya was Bulgarian, talk turned to holidays on the Black Sea coast. Most seemed to go there in the summer, as the legions of British toilers went to Spain. They talked and drank till closing time, when a fierce-faced barmaid turned everyone out into the cold night.

'Let us walk a little to clear our heads,' he suggested to Marya, 'We can get the *Strassenbahn* at *Oranienburger Tor.*'

It was a fine night, almost full-mooned, as they walked along Oranienburger Strasse. They passed the facade of the Jewish Synagogue, burned out in *Kristallnacht*. There was no Jewish community now in East Berlin and the ruin had been left as it was. On the wall was a memorial, telling of the destruction of the building in 1938. Further on in Grosse Hamburger Strasse was a cleared space, with another memento mori; here had stood an old folks home, which a wall plaque announced had been used as a clearing-house for the 'final solution'.

'That American, the journalist, it looks like what he said was right,' he thought to himself.

Marya shivered. 'Come on, let us keep walking to keep warm.'

They again passed quite near the Wall. The dazzle of light from the searchlights turned night to day. Further on, beside a white, angular building, an open gate led into what appeared to be a park.

'You do not know this place?' Marya asked. 'It is the *Brecht Haus*, where Brecht lived when he came back to the DDR. It is now a museum, or rather, a shrine. This is the *Dorotheenstadt* Cemetery. Brecht is buried here. Come, let us go inside, there is light enough.'

A wooden sign nailed to a tree was legible enough to indicate that the graveyard was closed, but the gate was unlocked. They went along a sandy path between the gravestones, some with cast-iron crosses on them. In the moonlight, they found Brecht's burial place. The scholar remembered the lines, '*Ich benötige keinen Grabstein...*' but he had one, nevertheless. Many others were buried there: Rausch, the sculptor of the statue of Frederick the Great that stood outside his library window, and Hegel, who noted that the owl of Minerva only flew after dusk had fallen – that we can only have understanding after the event.

Marya led him on to an overgrown corner and pulled back some branches. A cat scuttled across the path and disappeared. She looked up at him. He looked at the grave. There lay poor Heinrich, Thomas Mann's tortured and less exalted brother, who died on the way back to the DDR from Macarthyite America.

'He left it too long to make up his mind,' Marya said, allowing the branches to cover the bust of the writer again and turning to look at him.

They walked back to a small shelter and sat on a bench surrounded by the dead. She pulled him towards her for warmth. He listened for an owl in the graveyard where they sat, but none called.

Argentina Invades Falklands

Argentina today invaded and captured the Falkland Islands, overwhelming the small British garrison, a single company of Royal Marines, after a brief exchange of fire in the capital, Port Stanley. Cheering crowds gathered outside the Casa Rosada presidential palace in Buenos Aires to greet the head of the ruling military junta, General Galtieri, who said that "one of the last vestiges of imperialism" had been removed with the return of Las Malvinas to Argentina.

The Defence Secretary, John Nott, told a press conference that Britain was assembling a task force of up to 40 ships to retake the islands, but that it would be two weeks before it was ready to sail to the Falklands.

CHAPTER TWELVE

ONCE AGAIN HE found himself at Friedrichstrasse. After visiting the *Gepackausgabe*, he ascended to the platform and placed his briefcase on a bench. Then he bent down to tie a shoelace. The train came and he boarded it. It was not until the next station that he realised he had left the briefcase behind. He ran furiously through the underpass and waited on the opposite platform for a train back. It was five minutes before one came, but when he once again alighted at Friedrichstrasse he could see his case on the platform across the rails. Once more the rush down and up escalators until he stood, panting, at the bench. Surrounded by moving and stationary people, his case stood exactly where he had left it. Unsure whether he was glad to see it or not, he retraced his steps.

He spent the next week touring Berlin, his briefcase in his hand, his parcel in his briefcase, his heart in his mouth.

He visited the football stadium, the *Jahnpark*, to watch *Dynamo Berlin* against the team from Cottbus. The park was all-seated, and uncovered. Most spectators (the stadium was half full) carried holdalls, out of which they produced vacuum flasks and cushions. Inside the ground were a few *Volkspolizei*, but more striking were the group of *Grenzpolizei* with dogs patrolling the boundary of the stadium. The Wall ran directly behind the stadium and it might just have been possible to kick a ball into no-man's land. When the game started, the *Grenzpolizei* called their dogs to heel and watched.

The game was played with little flair and the crowd had not much to shout about. A group of well-behaved football hooligans stood on the benches behind one goal, chanting and waving scarves. Both times Berlin scored, they threw toilet rolls onto the cinder track which encircled the pitch. The police watched impassively as a group of FDJ youth picked up the toilet rolls and deposited them in plastic sacks. He wondered if they would try and recycle them; toilet paper was scarce.

Near to his flat was the VEB *Treppenbauwerke*, a medium-sized engineering works, with a convenient post-box on its front gate. Outside were the usual pictures of 'Worker of the Month' who had supposedly outfulfilled work norms and had no absences. He had heard it said that the state factories simply rotated the workforce members for this brief moment of fame. There was also a notice about the Brigade of the Month, so designated for its role in voluntary work at a local *Kindergarten* and its collective trips to the mountains and to the theatre. 'When did you last visit the theatre?' the Brigade leader asked accusingly of the other workers in the factory.

He went by train to the truck factory on the outskirts of Berlin. It was early and being the only non-worker on board he attracted attention. Those in the uniform of overalls looked like workers anywhere, though both less embourgeoisified or lumpenised than workers in the West. He could not follow much of the fast *Berlinisch* dialect, but the body language was international. The same camaraderie and humour allied to cynicism and gruffness, the international body language of the working class. Alone on the train back, he recalled all the many times he had done this in the West; the papermills, shipyards and engineering works he had visited at dawn, with leaflets and pamphlets about another dawn, and the good-humoured indifference that had greeted his efforts. He felt like the top half of an hourglass; everything was draining out. And when the bottom chamber was full, this glass would not be upturned for the sand to run again.

He went to Müggelsee, an area of wood and lake bordering the city, reached via Kopenick, where the Captain of Kopenick had led the Prussian Army and State a merry dance by donning the uniform of an Army officer. And here he was, another impostor, walking to the town hall where eighty years earlier the Captain had commandeered the cash-box.

At Müggelsee the natives ate, drank, skated and played at the amusement arcades. It was a frozen Blackpool, the lake still an unbroken pane of ice. After circling through the crowds he took himself off through the woods, where paths climbed the Müggelberg. Lost in the dense forest it was like some *Urwald*, and he half expected Siegfried to come crashing through the trees chasing after a boar. Here the German Army had made its last organised stand against the Red Army before retreating to fight in the streets of Berlin.

Accompanied only by the sound of his own footfalls and breathing, he walked off the path and, pushing branches aside, came to a clearing. Behind him he heard a branch crack. He turned to look and listen. Now that he was listening, he could hear the drumming of woodpeckers a little way off. Again, the snap of a branch, and into the clearing came a man who did not look like a forestry worker, but had had the unmistakable stamp of a *Beamte*.

He approached and asked in English, 'Which direction are you going? You seem a little off the path.'

He replied that he was heading for the Müggelberg, and the lookout point of the Müggelturm.

The stranger asked, 'Do you mind if I accompany you? I am going that way also.'

It seemed to be a point of information, not a question. The man's face was familiar. He had seen him before somewhere during that winter in Berlin.

They walked for a while in silence. Then the man offered, 'It is lovely here, really fresh. And soon it will be spring. It is also quiet here. The masses of people do not come this far; they do not care for lookout towers. Amusement arcades please them better.'

The scholar looked at his companion, who was wearing a *Kunstleder* coat, identical to those worn by the civil servants who crowded the Unter den Linden at rush hour. He was no Siegfried pursuing a wild boar. It was difficult to see him as threatening.

'Do you not wonder why I addressed you in English?'

'I know I look like an *Ausländer*,' was the reply.

'Yes, but an English, or rather, a Scottish *Ausländer*?'

He smiled the Mitropa smile, to inform his listener that he knew more than that simple fact.

They reached the *Müggelturm*, a lookout tower that rose to give a panoramic view of the *Märkisch* landscape of forest and lake.

Looking out over the sand fringed lakes and deep evergreen forest, his companion continued, 'It is a pity it is still winter.'

These words again: *noch Winter*.

'In summer from the tower it is a better view and I could have bought you a coffee in the restaurant at the top, which is sadly closed for the winter. But you have come to a reasonable lookout point; from here you can get quite a good view of our country. And you can almost see Poland; it is just over the horizon. But,' and again he smiled the same, ironical Mitropa smile, 'this is not Poland. The landscape is the same, but the social situation is different; here – thankfully – it is calm.'

The man waited for the words to sink in. Like the melting snow sinking into the ground.

The scholar asked, 'What do you want?'

The man paused for effect before answering. His impatient hearer noted that he would make a good actor.

'Want? We – I – do not want anything, unlike those who doubtless approach you from time to time for foreign currency, or other favours.' He continued, again after a pause, not taking his eyes from the landscape, 'No trouble, no fuss, no bother. We want you to enjoy your stay in the DDR, and to go home without any repercussions. I think that we understand one another, though yours is quite an unusual case. We have not had many like it before.'

'Why are you telling me this?'

'Why? Because we have nothing to gain from any incidents. And,' he continued, with a perceptible increase in emphasis, 'Neither have you. As I said, the situation here is calm. Any... gesture... would be meaningless. It is not 1953, or even 1961: the DDR is stable now.'

He smiled a slightly patronising smile. 'Now I must go. You can follow the path back to the Müggelsee quite easily. I hope you go home with pleasant memories of the DDR.'

And with that he descended and was soon out of sight. Out of the silence came the insistent sound of the woodpeckers.

Reagan Supports Iraq in War with Iran

In the heaviest fighting yet in the war with Iraq, Iran has made significant gains using human wave tactics against enemy positions, apparently at the cost of enormous casualties. In response to these setbacks, President Reagan has announced an increase in military and economic aid to the government of Saddam Hussein, stating that any extension of Iranian power in the Gulf region would not be in America's interests, given the hostility of the Islamic leaders in Teheran towards the U.S.A. Observers believe that, given the recent Iraqi reverses, U.S. aid is crucial to the survival of the Baghdad regime, which is by no means universally popular, resting as it does mainly on the Sunni minority to which Saddam and his allies largely belong.

CHAPTER THIRTEEN

MARYA SEEMED TO BE INTRIGUED by the prospect of a trip to the provinces. He had decided to go to Dresden, Weimar and Leipzig, and had picked up his visa for the whole country.

She suggested, 'When we return, you may have news of your application for an extension of your stay?'

He agreed that this was possible, though he knew it was not.

They took the train for Prague, moving south through the flat *Märkisch* landscape, until the scenery became more contoured as they entered Saxony. He was surprised to see vines.

'Yes, they make a white wine here, *Schaumwein*. It is fizzy. And very expensive, I think,' said Marya.

'Probably for export only,' he commented.

'You always manage to find fault,' she noted.

Soon they reached Dresden. They alighted. Near the

station was the stadium of the local football team; but he had had enough of football matches.

From the station to the town centre, Dresden had been rebuilt in 1950s Stalinist monumental style, large hotels, blocks of flats, a circular cinema, all in concrete. The first cameo they came to was the *Gewandhaus Hotel*, where they got a room. It was a reconstructed *Gasthof*, with heavy furniture, chandeliers and pastel-coloured plasterwork. He was asked by the receptionist if they were from '*sozialistischen Ausland oder capitalistischen Ausland*'. Payment varied according to this, the cheapest rates being for '*DDR Bürger*'. He handed over the two passports as an answer. The receptionist studied them, studied their owners and gave them a registration form to fill in.

Aware of what she was thinking, he tried to joke, 'I'm paying more. She can sleep on the floor and I'll have the bed.'

'I'm sure the bed will accommodate both of you,' was the sharp reply. The receptionist placed the passports in a drawer and handed them a room key. After washing, they went out to eat.

They walked towards the Elbe. The same river, but many miles upstream from Schönhausen. That trip now seemed long ago, as if belonging to another congerie of events. Now they were in reconstructed Dresden, where piece by piece, year by year, from plans and photographs, the town had been rebuilt after the Allied bombing raid – a raid that had killed more people than the attack on Hiroshima. He meditated on the cost-effectiveness of incinerating people in air raids, rather than in concentration camps.

The beauty of the city surprised him. It was an un-German beauty that had inspired Canaletto to depict it to look Venetian. Reproductions of the artist's works were on sale at all the evening-closed shops. The royal palace had been rebuilt, the Zwinger and the Semper Opera House were being reconstructed. Only in the city centre did a ruined church remain as a reminder of the war. On the other side of the river, beside the gold statue of Augustus, who left to become King of Poland, they were amongst restored *Bürger* houses, and found a restaurant. Later they went to the *Dresdner Philharmonie* and walked back to the *Gewandhaus* by the dark Elbe. It was milder; spring was on the way. They came to the *Fürstenzug*, a ceramic display of the rulers of Saxony through the ages.

As he surveyed it tipsily and cheerfully, he commented to Marya, 'You know, I am not a very serious person. Most of all I like touristic activities, with a little culture thrown in. When I was younger I was an intellectual; now I am only a person of culture.'

'Very few people are even that,' she replied. 'Thinking otherwise is your big mistake.'

Next day they moved on. In the carriage opposite them two girls practised their French. The train travelled through rolling, wooded countryside. Weimar. The town of classical German literature, adoptive home of Goethe and Schiller. The town where the German parliament met after 1918 because Berlin was too 'red'. The station was a subterranean cavern under the track, dimly lit and tiled yellow. Some African students were hanging about at a snack bar looking bored. Outside, bare trees, dusty streets and faded tenements. The station was a little out of town and they walked towards the centre. Now they were in a world of restored roccoco houses, pastel-coloured, with shops selling prints and ceramics. It was like an open-air museum. They took a little walk to Goethe's *Gartenhaus* in a park by the river. Here he spent the summers almost within sight of his town house; no cultural tourist he.

'I think we should look for somewhere to stay,' said Marya. 'Sometimes accommodation can be difficult, and I only noticed one hotel. Let's go back there.'

And back through the tiny urban museum they strolled to the hotel, where disappointment awaited. Due to a conference on the Classical German Tradition in Literature, the hotel was full. But the receptionist took pity on them and rang up a Youth Hostel – he winced – on the outskirts of town, where she asked for, and got, accommodation for '*zwei junge Leute*'. It was a little out of town, she said, but there would be a bus in an hour. Meanwhile they could eat in the restaurant. Where was the hostel, he asked?

'Buchenwald.'

Buchenwald. The beechwood. A word known to many by its historical associations, whose knowledge of its literal meaning was limited. He looked at Marya to see if the name made an impact on her. She remained impassive. Maybe, he thought, there is more than one beech wood in Germany.

'Let's go to eat,' she insisted.

As they entered the hotel restaurant, the entire clientele rose to their feet and began clapping. Their entry was evidently the cause of the celebration.

'Why are they clapping?' he asked Marya, relying on her knowledge of Eastern European ritual.

'They probably think we are delegates to the conference,' she replied. 'Just smile politely and they will sit down.'

He followed her advice and order was restored. They ate, then returned to the station to collect their luggage and wait for the bus. An old woman stood at the bus stop. He asked her when the bus to Buchenwald would come.

'*Bald, bald,*' she said, and then, with the unfailing curiosity he had come to expect, asked him where he came from, what he was doing in the DDR and so on.

In response, unbidden, she informed him, '*Ich bin nicht hier geboren. Stamm aus Sudentenland.*'

She had been expelled by the Czechs in 1945. What things had she seen, he wondered, what did she think of her enforced adoptive homeland? About these things she did not speak and he did not ask. But he knew why she could wait so patiently for a bus. It finally came. The road climbed through woods, beech woods and past a watch factory on the outskirts of the town, illuminated in neon. Past a memorial on their left and a ruined rail-siding on their right. Confirmation at every turn of what he feared. Buchenwald was not a village, only the camp.

They got out when the bus halted, as did some teenagers with no luggage, who were probably staying at the hostel. The camp was ahead, its wall topped by barbed wire, its watchtowers visible, though unilluminated. The teenagers went towards a group of buildings that reminded him of the pictures he had seen of the agricultural *Siedlungen* of the Third Reich. In front of the buildings were two signs: *Jugendherberge* read the first, SS *Kaserne* the second. They pointed in the same direction. To the quarters of the men who had killed as a matter of routine, tortured out of boredom or for physical pleasure.

Neither he nor Marya spoke. He knew what lay ahead. Years before, with a previous companion, he had left Munich on a grey day, to drive to Dachau. The village was a clean and well-lit place, an advert for the *Wirtschaftswunder*. Here the communists who held Munich in 1919 had fought with the Reichswehr advancing on the city, though he and his companion were probably the only people visiting Dachau who knew that. And no signs to the camp. They asked one or two local people who either shrugged their shoulders in incomprehension or claimed they did not know. A drunk, staggering on the pavement, heard them asking directions and approached, filling the car with alcohol fumes as he jutted his head through the rolled-down window.

'*Dachau? Sie wollen Dachau?*' He opened the back door, uninvited, and deposited himself in the seat. Every now and then he would leap forward, interrupting his own drunken monologue, with shouts of '*rechts*' or '*links*', until they left the village behind and entered the well-ordered Bavarian countryside. Huge farm steadings everywhere, with window-boxes draped with flowers. They began to suspect that the drunk was stealing a lift home, but at another '*links*', they saw a car park, full of tourist buses. They parked and his companion said she would wait in the car.

'You have to know about these things,' he insisted.

'I know. I will wait,' she repeated.

He offered his new acquaintance a lift back to Dachau village, if he too would wait. Staggering about and waving his arm, he rejected the offer. He began to laugh soundlessly. Then spoke.

'You know why… you know why they did not destroy this place after the last war? You know why, eh?' He waited but no reply was forthcoming. 'Because they are keeping it for the next time!'

He turned, and was gone.

Arbeit Macht Frei: a squalid little piece of blacksmith's work above an undistinguished gate. From here they had gone forth to work in the fields and quarries, to be worked to deliberate death. But no one had seen them, they had been invisible. He knew what lay ahead.

The schoolchildren and their teacher occupied one barracks. In this unseasonable month for visitors, he and Marya were given a separate barracks, not occupied by anyone else. They were given separate rooms, but he knew she would come. Long corridors gave onto individual rooms, whose fitments looked original, antiseptic. Here the torturers had washed, urinated, scratched themselves, read *Der Stürmer*. There was no adequate response, nor could there be any point in looking for one.

'It was cold,' she said, repeating the words of the first night, as she came and began to touch him.

He tried to be unresponsive.

'Let's not bother, not tonight, not here.'

'Don't be so theatrical,' she insisted.

After the mouth, lips and teeth made the words, they

made contact with his body. Guiltily, he willed himself to stay inert, but failed.

'Lie still!' she hissed, and moved over him.

She rose and fell on him slowly, with closed eyes. He did nothing till she eventually slumped down onto him. He spent a troubled night in a murderer's room.

Martial Law Relaxed in Poland

Martial Law has been relaxed in Poland. The curfew has been lifted, as well as the ban on public entertainments. Several thousand political prisoners, about one-third of the total, have been released. The government has stated that it hopes these measures will allow the process of a dialogue to begin in the country, in a situation of stability and based on a political realism removed from the "verge of the abyss" where the country had stood six months ago. Whilst Pope John Paul has welcomed the measures, there has been no reaction so far from Solidarity leaders, either those still in custody or those working underground.

CHAPTER FOURTEEN

LEIPZIG WAS THEIR last stop. Here there was no difficulty with hotels, geared as the city was to trade and book fairs. Leipzig looked more Western to his eyes; there were more cars, more adverts. They went to St Thomas's, walking over Bach's memorial gravestone on the pavement outside the *Kirche*. On the noticeboard was a handbill advertising the meetings of a support group for homosexuals. Inside, a dress rehearsal of the cantata '*Ein' feste Burg ist unser Gott*' was taking place. Bach himself had probably never heard it so well performed; nor had the scholar, who listened for an hour while Marya walked around Leipzig.

The performance was part of a celebration of the 500th anniversary of Luther's birth: the reformer had penned the words later set to music by Bach. An exhibition in the church announced 'In the DDR Luther's Contribution will be Honoured!' The scholar was looking through the exhibits on the Peasants' War and on Luther's theology, when a young *Pfarrer* approached him.

'You are interested in the exhibition? Are you a Protestant?'

He replied that he was not, though he had been brought up one.

'But I am interested in the exhibition. You say here,' – pointing to a leaflet – 'that the Church is in "critical solidarity" with the DDR state. How do you justify that?'

The Mitropa smile again.

'Well, the state helps a lot with restoration projects of an ecclesiastical nature, and with exhibitions like this... and it does not oppose churchgoing. We actually have higher church attendance rates than in the West...'

'But the Wall?'

'The Wall is evil, but it prevents evil. There is no real chance to sin in the DDR. Crime, pornography, violence, racial hatred – the Wall prevents them, keeps them out. It makes my job easier...'

'People are hibernating from sin?'

'If you like, yes.'

'What if they waken up?'

The *Pfarrer* smiled an open smile, 'Oh, I don't think that will happen.'

Marya had returned and was looking impatient, so he thanked the *Pfarrer* and ended the discussion.

Outside, after walking a short distance, his eye caught a sign above a basement restaurant.

In boyish delight he cried out, *'Auerbachs Keller.* It is where Faust went after selling his soul to Mephistopheles. Let's go there to eat. Come!'

The restaurant was furnished in a late nineteenth-century restoration style. On the walls was a frieze of the main scenes from the *Faust* drama. The waiters were dressed in long white pinafores. As they drank the dark, nutty local beer in big glass bowls, he deciphered the various inscriptions above the murals. '*Der wer immer strebt*', wasn't that how it went? He who ever strives, that man we can save, Goethe had said. And here he was, his strivings degenerated into touristic pleasures. But, what the hell, he thought, as the alcohol hit its target; he would rather make love to Marya than be a martyr in Buchenwald. They spent the evening in the cavernous restaurant, eating, drinking, talking. Marya again mentioned his application to stay longer in the DDR. Did she believe him or not? He ordered another beer.

He thought of Turgenev's maxim that all men are either Hamlet or Don Quixote, either ineffectively reflective or ineffectively impulsive. Faust, however, united both the reflective and impulsive tendencies and was the more significant figure. But Faust's impulses were empty gestures, his reflections arid. Marya asked what he was thinking about.

'Oh, about Faust,' he said tipsily, smiling. 'And how I am just like him. Except that no one wants to buy my soul. Not even the Devil.'

'And am I to be your Gretchen, abandoned and dishonoured?' came the riposte, mock-serious.

'But remember, you redeem me and we are reconciled, *im Zweiter Teil*,' he quipped, deflecting the sally.

'Will there be a second part to this story?' she asked.

'It depends on you. But maybe it's time to stop living your

life through a series of references to books, and to do something.' When he did not reply, she continued, 'Come, let us go back to the hotel.'

In the room, silence. Marya lay on the bed, looking at the same spot on the roof. He switched on the radio, to fill the void. They listened to a Big Band concert on the US Armed Forces Network. Then came a news bulletin. He listened indifferently and then stunned as the newscaster spoke.

Today the newspapers of the Axel Springer press have published a leaflet, said to have been distributed in the DDR. The leaflet calls for strikes by workers in the DDR in support of the workers in Poland suffering under martial law. The leaflets said the DDR was state capitalism and not communism, and its regime had to be overthrown by the workers. It is claimed that these leaflets show the operation of an organised underground movement in the DDR. No one from the official news agency ADN would comment, and nothing about these leaflets has appeared in the official newspaper, Neues Deutschland.

The British Naval task force has arrived in the South Atlantic in response to the Argentinian occupation of the Falkland Islands, or Malvinas…

Marya rose and switched off the radio. She came over to where he stood by the window, looked at him and then out of the window before she spoke.

'You got some more leaflets from abroad?'

'Yes.'

'But you said you would try and get permission to stay here, so why...?'

'I lied. I can't stay here. I must go back home. A relationship between us is not possible, there or here.' He moved from the window to the bed and lay down. 'There is nothing to be done. But you must say you knew nothing, nothing at all. I'll say the same. If they think you know anything you'll probably end up in the People's Heroic Yoghurt Works, or something.'

She did not smile at his weak attempt at humour.

'I don't think we have to worry about me,' she intimated pointedly. He was surprised at how calmly she appeared to be taking events. And then she added, getting up to leave, 'I will wait downstairs. And do not be over-anxious. The *Stasi* are not the Gestapo.'

'I know that. If they had been, I would not be here. You know that.'

But she did not seem to be listening as she went out of the door.

He had only to wait about half an hour. When he opened the door, the larger of the two men smiled, the smaller scowled. Good cop, bad cop, thought the scholar. They've seen the film.

'*Sicherheitspolizei*,' the latter stated, showing a badge with the DDR logo. 'We would like you to come with us, to answer some questions.'

'Why?' he asked.

'We are not allowed to say. Please come without any fuss. Just come as you are. Your things will be collected and brought to you.'

'And my passport?'

'We already have your passport.'

He was led down the stairs and out of the hotel. Two cars, with drivers, were waiting at the pavement. Marya stood beside one of them.

'Goodbye, Marya.'

She turned away without answering and entered one of the cars. He got in the other with the two *Sicherheitspolizei*.

'Where is she going?' he asked.

'That does not concern you. You have more important things to think about now. In the DDR we do not take kindly to criminal attempts to undermine the state,' answered one of his escorts.

They drove. They drove in darkness, and in silence. From the road signs he could tell that they were headed north.

'Where are we going?'

'Berlin. But that will not be the end of your journey. I think you will be getting to know some of the remoter parts of our republic before long, as a guest of our government,' the taller policeman responded.

Then he seemed to relent a little.

'You really are a mug. What did you think you could achieve? Germans don't make revolutions, especially the well-fed ones we have here. Listen, I will give you some advice. We could jail you for fifteen years for this. And don't think your government would try too hard to get you out. If you want to go home soon, co-operate. They might have a suggestion to make, so don't play the hero; there isn't an audience.'

A couple of hours later they were on the outskirts of the *Hauptstadt der* DDR, the familiar landmarks of the TV mast at Alexanderplatz and the Storkower Strasse water tower standing out above the flat plain of buildings. To his surprise, the car drove down the Unter den Linden, to the University.

For a while they sat in the car saying nothing, then the tall policeman said, 'Go and see your *Betreuer*, she is expecting you. We will wait here. You will not run away, we have your passport,' he smiled. 'When you have discussed with her the termination of your studies here, come back and we can decide where to go. Either a short trip to West Berlin, or a longer one to the *Sicherheitspolizei* headquarters. Now go, and remember what I said, co-operate.'

He got out of the car, crossed the pavement and entered the University.

PM Rejoices as South Georgia is Recaptured

Royal Marines today recaptured South Georgia, the island invaded by Argentina four weeks ago. An elite Special Boat Squadron landed on the island and crossed the frozen mountain range to attack the Argentinians at the old whaling base of Grytviken. The Defence Secretary said there was limited Argentine resistance and no British casualties. The Prime Minister said, "Let us congratulate our armed forces. Rejoice! Rejoice!"

In the wake of the Falklands crisis, opinion polls show Mrs Thatcher's popularity soaring. Similar surveys earlier in the year, in the wake of rising unemployment figures, recorded her as the least popular British Prime Minister in history.

CHAPTER FIFTEEN

ONCE AGAIN THE BROAD STAIRWAY, the bust of Liebknecht, the linoleum corridor. He entered the room of his *Betreuer*. She was sitting at her desk.

'I hope you have had a good journey, and learned a little about life in our country?' she greeted him. 'I have not been a very good *Betreuer*, I am afraid. But tell me, what has been the outcome of your scholarly studies, what conclusions have you come to about Bismarck?'

Disarmed by the turn of the conversation, he re-armed himself with a rebuff.

'You already know what I have discovered about Bismarck. And I have not come here to discuss that.'

She looked at him as if she had not heard him.

'What interested me about your Bismarck studies was your methodology. The idea that one has to make a realistic choice between possible alternatives and not dream about a third, optimum possibility for historical evolution.'

She paused, as if considering this. 'Why do you not apply this to society in general? Why do you not look at what is possible and choose the best, even the lesser of two evils, rather than the futile pursuit of the impossible?'

'That is just a convenient argument for reconciliation to power and exploitation. We can only know in retrospect what the real choices were, not today. So we have to act on the basis of our desires.'

'I do not think that is consistent. We have to choose, but we cannot choose our choices, these are given to us. If we can only be realistic in retrospect, how did Bismarck know at the time, the only realistic route to German unification?' After a short pause, Dr Feld started talking again. 'I will tell you a story. In 1953 I was a student at this University. I supported the foundation of the DDR, but hated Stalinism. I was very influenced by the works of Rosa Luxemburg, with which I am sure you are familiar?'

He indicated that he was.

'One day I left the University and was walking along the Unter den Linden much of which was still in ruins after the war. The place was thronged with building workers from the housing projects on Stalin-Allee who had struck against the new work norms. But again, I am sure you are familiar with the events of 1953 here in Berlin?'

He did not contradict the familiarity assumed.

'I joined the demonstration, as did other passers-by, as it headed for the Brandenburg Gate – there was no Wall at that time, of course. People were unsure what to do. The government under Ulbricht had foolishly refused to speak to the strikers, and some suggested that we go to the Western sector to have our demands broadcast on the American army radio station. A man jumped onto the back of a lorry and began to argue for such a course of action. As he talked, he raised his arm. His shirt slipped and I could see the ss identification number tattooed on his arm. He had been working in a penal battalion like many others of his kind and had managed to gain an influence in events.'

She paused for this to have its effect.

He retorted angrily now, 'But the presence of a few Nazis does not discredit the demands of the workers, which were just. That is just a convenient way of avoiding the issue. And it sounds to me like the kind of tale you learn in Party-school, for propaganda purposes.'

She sighed, continued, 'No, the story is true. I did not go to the Western sector with the strikers. Then of course, the Russian tanks came and the demonstrations were dispersed.' She looked at the desk a while, twirling a pencil in her hand. Then she looked up, her face tired. 'Yes, the demands of the workers were just. And I am sure many of the demands in Poland are just, too. But in the context of those times they could only serve the interests of fascist revanchism and us imperialism. The Party here corrected its mistakes and hopefully the Party in Poland will do so as well. But if the Party lost its grip, the alternative would not be the Utopia you seek, but the restoration of capitalism.'

Silence returned. He thought she had finished but she began again after a few moments.

'Communism today stands in the position of the Reformation at the end of the seventeenth century. At first the revolutionary impulses of Protestantism and Communism both seemed to be about to sweep all before them. But the forces opposed to them organised a counter-reformation in one case, a counter-revolution in the other. In the end both of these revolutionary impulses had to be content with the smaller, and poorer, part of the spoils. And in the process both Protestantism and Communism turned against and devoured their own radical children, and their best ideals, as they became compromised state systems. And in both cases state-Protestantism and state-communism, were the only alternatives, but still progressive. It is possible for someone here in the DDR to support the system without being an *Apparatschnik*, though these exist in plenty, because there is only the alternative of the West.'

He could see she still had not finished and began to think that she was talking more to herself than to him.

'Tell me, you are from Scotland. Do you know the historical novels of Walter Scott? Yes? A profound dialectician, as Lukács said, even if Scott was a Tory. Scott for me expresses the tragic nature of the historical human condition and the impossibility of Utopia. Forces clash, and in their resolution a seedy compromise is patched up, that betrays the idealists and favours the toadies and time-servers. But for most people, this new synthesis is better than what went before. You Utopians who think there is a real alternative, can remind us of how far we have compromised our ideals, even jolt us into some kind of reform. But what you want today is no more possible than what the Anabaptists wanted in the Reformation. You must, as I said, generalise your Bismarck method, apply it to reality today. And life in the DDR is not too bad. No unemployment, no homelessness, no drugs, little crime...'

'No democracy and no equality either. If you had these there would be no need for a Wall to keep your citizens from defecting. But why am I talking to you and not the police, unless you are the police? What do you want? Not just to give an airing to your bad conscience, surely?'

Dr Feld fingered her pencil again and studied the familiar surface of her desk.

'Democracy? If we give them democracy before we can give them BMWs, they will vote for capitalism. That is what they want, not the cheap culture which you have enjoyed during your stay. But on your other point, I am not the police, although every DDR citizen has a duty to be vigilant in defense of the state, with all its flaws.' She continued mechanically, 'We know that the Director at the Cultural Mission here – who took you to the revanchist *Gesamtdeutsche Institut* – knew about the plans of your small band of Utopians to aid the Polish workers by trying to induce in the DDR the chaos that has brought Poland low. We know about the mail to the Mission. We did not want an issue over this, that could serve us no purpose. But for some reason Springer gained a copy of your leaflet. We think your Director friend was responsible. The proposal is this. We would like to publish an interview with you saying you regret what you have done. In return you will be out of DDR territory within an hour. But you must sign this transcript.'

She pushed a document, in question-and-answer form, towards him and pointed to where he was to sign.

'What if I do not agree?'

She shrugged her shoulders.

'I imagine there will be a trial, then you will be expelled. We do not want to keep you, you are no use to us: your own government would not want to exchange anyone of ours they hold for you.' She pushed the text forward. 'What do you say?'

'I cannot do that. I cannot put my name to that,' he said.

Dr Feld nodded. 'I did not think you would agree. And the trial was a bluff. We do not want you making speeches that Springer would print and the US radio relay to our population. Go back to the car outside and tell them all went well. They will know what to do.'

She stood up and held out her hand.

'Good luck. I look forward to reading your publication on Bismarck. You will send me a copy?'

After a hesitation, he took the hand and promised to do so. He knew he would write the work, knew it would be good. It would be a success of the trip. Yet he was aware that the other motive in his coming also had a successful outcome: millions in the DDR, listening to Western television and radio, knew about the leaflet – but due to the Director and to Springer, not to himself.

'*Alles gut?*' asked the taller *Sicherheitspolizist*.

'*Alles gut*. I think we go to the border now, don't we?'

They drove down Unter den Linden. He noted that the linden trees, felled by the Nazis, replanted by the Stalinists, were in bud, though not in bloom. It was no longer winter. They turned into Friedrichstrasse, towards the border crossing point, where he had crossed before, with Marya. They went again to the diplomatic lane.

The policeman handed him his passport and told him, as he got out of the car, 'As you go through border control, you will be given your possessions.'

He found himself on the pavement, looking around. The checkpoint was surrounded by derelict buildings, gap-windowed and roofless, left to disguise the wall from Eastern eyes. Reliefs of figures carved in one ruined building caught his attention and he had to smile. The final irony arranged by the director of this whole drama. The heroes of the war of unification, Moltke and William II, presided over by Bismarck, glowered down at him from the ruins; from the sepulchre of history.

He walked to the crossing point and presented his passport. The DDR border guard produced from under the counter the suitcase he had last seen in Leipzig, as well as his suitcase from the Pankow flat, and asked him to examine these and sign for his belongings. He signed without checking.

'*Wollen Sie nicht prüfen?*' the guard queried.

'*Nein. Nicht nötig.*'

Out towards the white line across the road, crossing it and his own shadow line. From the American control barrier, soldiers watched with binoculars. Behind them were the crowds of tourists at the Checkpoint Charlie Museum, photographing the Wall, the towers and the *Grenzpolizei.* The wall was covered with graffiti. One slogan read 'Behind here, unreality'. He showed his passport to the US official at the barrier. He rested his case on the ground and looked to the East. He thought of Dr Feld, and of Marya. He received his passport back.

He picked up his case and walked again forward, back to the West. The newspaper billboards spoke of the British-Argentine war over the Falklands and diplomatic expulsions between the DDR and the UK.

It was warm. The season of hibernation was over. It was spring in Berlin.

Glossary of German Words and Phrases

WORDS

Alltagsleben: everyday life
Apfel: apple
Apparatchiks: apparatchik (an agent of the apparatus)
Ausgang: exit
ausverkauft: sold out
bald: soon
Bärenblut: blood of a bear
Beamte: official
Berlinisch: Berlin dialect
Betreuer: academic supervisor
Bibliothek: library
Bibliothekskarte: library card
Bier: beer
Branntwein: brandy
Braunkohle: lignite, low-grade coal
DDR: Deutsche Demokratische Republik
Delikatessen: delikatessen
Denkmal: monument
Distel: thistle
Eingang: entrance
entschuldigung: excuse me
Erbsen-suppe: pea soup
FDJ (*Freie Deutsche Jugend*): Free German Youth – Communist
Youth Organisation)
Flüchtling: refugee
Garderobe: cloakroom
Gastarbeiter: immigrant worker
Gaststätte: restaurant
Gebratene Ente: roast duck
Geburtsort: birthplace
gemütlich: comfortable, pleasant
Geschichte: history
Gepäckannahme: luggage office
Grenze: border
Grenzpolizei: border police of the DDR

Grenzpolizist (*Grenzpo*): border policeman
Grenzübergang: border checkpoint
Grossbritannien: Great Britain
Gummis: contaceptives
hingerichtet: executed
interessant: interesting
ja: yes
Jugendherberge: youth hostel
Kalbsbraten: roast veal
Kapitaisches Ausland: DDR term for non Eastern-bloc countries
Kaserne: barracks
Kaufhalle: small supermarket
Kino: cinema
Kirche: church
Kneipe: working-class pub
komm: come
Kulturclub: arts club
Kunstleder: imitation leather
langweilig: boring, dull
Machtergreifung: Hitler's seizure of power, 1933
Mark: German Mark
Märkisch: old Prussian architecture, culture etc
Die Mauer: the Berlin wall
Morgen: morning
nein: no
Novelle: novel
Ofen: stove
Osten: east
Ost-Elbisch: East-Elbian
Ostmark: East German currency
Pfarrer: Protestant clergyman
Ratskeller: basement restaurant
Realpolitik: realistic politics
Reichsbahn: railway
Reisepass: passport
Roman: novel
Rundfahrt: round trip

S-Bahn: suburban train
Schloss: mansion
Schwarzbrot: dark rye bread
SED (Socialistische Einheitspartei Deutschlands): Socialist Unity
Party of Germany (Communist Party)
Siedlung: housing scheme
Siegesäule: Memorial to Bismark
Stadtmitte: town centre
Stasi (Staatsicherheitspolizei): Secret Police (of DDR)
stempeln: to stamp, validate
Strassenbahn: tram, trolleybus
Tiergarten: zoo
U-Bahn: metro
Unterbringung: dormitory accommodation
vielleicht: maybe
Volksarmee: People's Army of the DDR
Volkspolizisten (Vopos): People's Police of the DDR
Vorsicht: caution, attention
Wende: turning point
Westmark: West German Mark
Wirtschaftswunder: economic miracle
Witze: joke, witticism
wohin: whither, where to
Zucker: sugar

PHRASES

CHAPTER I
Es ist noch Winter in Berlin. It is still winter in Berlin.
Bis Morgen. Acht Uhr. Punkt. See you tomorrow. Eight o'clock.
On the dot.
Sie gehen nach Berlin? Are you going to Berlin?
Nein, ich gehe nach Ost Berlin. Um zu studieren. No, I'm going
to East Berlin. To study.
Sie waren in Amerika? You were in America?
Gute Reise. Have a good trip.
Auch interessant. Also interesting.

Bleiben sie ruhig. Sie sind in West Berlin. Stay calm. You are in West Berlin.

Immer noch West Berlin. Still West Berlin.

Bitte einsteigen. Please embark.

Berlin, Hauptstadt der DDR. Wilkommen! Berlin, capital of the DDR. Welcome!

Zeitschrift für Geschichtswissenschaft magazine of historical scholarship

Gut, gut bekleidet. Es ist noch Winter in Berlin. It's good you're well clad. It's still winter in Berlin.

CHAPTER 2

Unterbringung der Humboldt Universität Humboldt University accommodation.

Real existierender Sozialismus Socialism as it really exists. Term used by the SED to describe the economic stage the DDR had achieved in the 1980s.

Sie müssen stempeln. You must get it stamped.

CHAPTER 3

Sie kommen Bismarck zu studieren. You've come to study Bismarck.

Bei uns sind diese Sachen wichtig. In our country these things are important.

Sektion Geschichte. History Section

Hier. Für Sie. Here. For you.

Diese Karte zeigt die alten Grenzen. This map shows the old borders.

Ja, ja. Alte Karte, alte Grenzen. Yes, yes. Old map, old borders.

Statistisches Jahrbuch für das Deutsche Reich. Statistical Yearbook for Germany

Nicht weiter. Nicht gestattet. No further. Not allowed.

Ja, natürlich. Yes, of course.

CHAPTER 4

Zwanzig Pfennig. Twenty pence.

Nein, nein. Tagesmenü. No, no. The menu of the day.

Kalbsbraten mit Sauerkraut. Roast veal with sauerkraut.
Noch ein Bier bitte. Another beer, please.
Ist dieser Platz noch frei? Is this seat free?
Hier in der DDR *haben wir keine wirkliche Freiheit.* Here in the
DDR there's no real freedom.
Zu Beishel. (zum Beispiel? For example)
Was ist denn los? What's the matter?
Zu viel, zu viel! Too much, too much!
Jetz gehe ich. I'm off now.
Es ist so kalt. Ich habe keinen Ofen. It's so cold. I don't have a
stove.
Haben Sie Zucker? Do you have any sugar?
Nein. Aber ich habe Whisky. Wollen Sie trinken? No. But I have
some whisky. Would you like a drink?

CHAPTER 5
Verschönert unsere hauptstadt Berlin! *Alles für das wohl
des Volkes und das glück der Kinder*! Beautify our capital,
Berlin. Everything for the people's wellbeing and the children's
happiness.

CHAPTER 6
Orangen aus Kuba. Cuban Oranges
Mir war kalt. Hier ist es wärmer. I was cold. It's warmer here.
Zu kalt um zu warten. Too cold to wait.
gebratene Ente: roast duck
Und nichts anders. And nothing else
Noch nicht. Not yet.
Was möchten Sie? What would you like?
Zwei Kaffee... und zwei Whisky. Two coffees... and two whiskies.
So viele Gummis für einen Tag. So many condoms for one day.

CHAPTER 7
'*Ballade von der sexuellen Hörigkeit*' 'Ballad of Sexual
Obedience' (Brecht–Weill)

CHAPTER 8

Ja, über Berlin weiss ich bescheid. Yes, I know about Berlin.
Die Kirche? Ja, warte fünf minuten. The church? Yes, wait five minutes.

CHAPTER 9

Man sieht die im Lichte, die im Dunkeln sieht man nicht.
You see those in the light, those in the darkness you don't see.
Eine Stunde oder eine Nacht? An hour or a night?

CHAPTER 11

Ich habe zu viel gearbeitet. I have been working too much.
Sie waren in West Berlin? You were in West Berlin?
Dort haben sie mehr Geld, aber hier ist das Leben gemütlicher.'
They have more money there, but life is more comfortable here.
Sektion Geschichte. History Section.
So, alles ist gemütlich? So, everything is cosy?
Berlin bleibt rot! Berlin remains red!
Sie sind aus dem Westen. You come from the West.
Und Sie finden das Leben hier angenehm? And you find life here
pleasant?
Ich benötige keinen Grabstein. I don't need any gravestone.

CHAPTER 13

Ich bin nicht hier geboren. Stamm aus Sudentenland.
I wasn't born here. I come from Sudetenland.

CHAPTER 15

Wollen Sie nicht prüfen? Don't you want to check.
Nein, Nicht nötig. No. Not neccessary.

Some Key Historical Figures

Arafat, Yasser (1929–2004) Chairman of the Palestinian Liberation Organisation

Bismarck, Otto von (1815–98) first chancellor of the German empire

Brecht, Bertolt (1898–1956) leftist poet, playwright and theatre director

Honecker, Erich (1912–1994) East German leader 1971–89

Jaruzelski, Wojciech (1923—) former Polish communist leader

Lenin, Vladimir Ilyich (1870–1924) Bolshevik leader of the Russian October Revolution

Mann, Thomas (1875–1955) novelist and essayist, 1929 Nobel Laureate

Mann, Heinrich (1871–1950) novelist, exiled from Germany in 1933

Marx, Karl (1818–1883) German political economist and theorist, philosopher, communist and revolutionary

May, Gisela (1924—) leading performer of Brecht's work

Monk, Thelonious (1917–82) American jazz pianist and composer

Liebknecht, Karl (1871–1919) founder of the Communist Party of Germany

Stalin, Joseph (1878–1953) Russian leader who ruthlessly purged his opponents

Weill, Kurt (1900–50) composer, collaborator with Bertolt Brecht

Mountain Outlaw
Ian R Mitchell
ISBN 1 84282 027 3 PBK £6.50

The amazing story of Ewan Macphee, Scotland's last bandit – some describe him as Scotland's answer to Ned Kelly. In 1850 Ewan MacPhee, these islands' last outlaw, died awaiting trial in jail in Fort William. MacPhee has fascinated Ian R Mitchell for many years. He has sifted the surviving information on the outlaw, examined many of the legends associated with him, bridged the gaps with an imagination of great authenticity, to produce *Mountain Outlaw*, a historical–creative account of MacPhee's life.

MacPhee lived in the era of steamships, railways and scientific advance, when traditional Highland society had all but disappeared. The tale of his lonely and ultimately hopeless fight against the modern world illuminates his epoch.

...it is fascinating, indeed, to decide what real and what is less or more so, to separate the fict from the faction, or vice versa. All in all, it's an astounding story, intricately told.
THE DAILY MAIL

This City Now: Glasgow and its working class past
Ian R Mitchell
ISBN 1 84282 082 6 PBK £12.99

This City Now sets out to retrieve the hidden architectural, cultural and historical riches of some of Glasgow's working-class districts. Many who enjoy the fruits of Glasgow's recent gentrification will be surprised and delighted by the gems which Ian Mitchell has uncovered beyond the usual haunts.

An enthusiastic walker and historian, Mitchell invites us to recapture the social and political history of the working-class in Glasgow, by taking us on a journey from Partick to Rutherglen, and Clydebank to Pollokshaws, revealing the buildings which go unnoticed every day yet are worthy of so much more attention. You will never walk through Glasgow in the same way again.

...both visitors and locals can gain instruction and pleasure from this fine volume...Mitchell is a knowledgable, witty and affable guide through the streets of the city.
GREEN LEFT WEEKLY

Scotland's Mountains before the Mountaineers

Ian R Mitchell
ISBN 0 946487 39 1 £9.99

In this groundbreaking book, Ian Mitchell tells the story of explorations and ascents in the Scottish Highlands in the days before mountaineering became a popular sport – when Jacobites, bandits, poachers and illicit distillers traditionally used the mountain as sanctuary.

Scotland's Mountains before the Mountaineers is divided into four Highland regions, with a map of each region showing key summits. While not designed primarily as a guide, it is nevertheless a useful handbook for walkers and climbers.

Based on a wealth of new research, this book offers a fresh perspective that will fascinate climbers and mountaineers, and anyone interested in the history of mountaineering, cartography, the evolution of the landscape and the social history of the Scottish Highlands.

Walking through Scotland's History: Two thousand years on foot

Ian R Mitchell
ISBN 1 905222 44 0 PBK £7.99

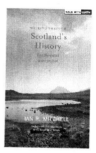

Today, walking is many things for many people – a leisure activity, a weekend pursuit, or even a chore – but rarely is it an integral part of everyday life. This book explores the world, and the way of life, that Scotland has left behind.

From the Roman legions marching into Caledonia, to the 20th century's travelling communities, Ian R Mitchell takes up on a tour of the missionaries, mapmakers and military leaders who have trodden Scottish paths over the last 2,000 years. He also examines the lives of the drovers, distillers, fishwives and workers for whom walking was a means of survival.

This new edition includes a variety of suggested walks and places to visit for each chapter, as an incentive for those who wish to follow in the footsteps of history.

Mountain Days and Bothy Nights

Dave Brown and Ian R Mitchell
ISBN 1 906307 83 0 PBK £7.50

*One thing we'll pit intae it is that
there's mair tae it than trudging up and
doon daft wet hills.*

This classic 'bothy book' celebrates
everything there is to hillwalking;
the people who do it, the stories they
tell and the places they sleep. Where
bothies came from, the legendary
walkers, the mountain craftsmen and
the Goretex and gaiters brigade – and
the best and the worst of the dosses,
howffs and bothies of the Scottish
hills.

The book itself has now become part
of the legends of the hills. Still likely
to inspire you to get out there with a
sleeping bag and a hipflask, this new
edition brings a bit of mountaineering
history to the modern Munro
bagger. The climbers dossing down
under the corries of Lochnagar may
have changed in dress, politics and
equipment, but the mountains and the
stories are timeless.

A View from the Ridge

Dave Brown and Ian R Mitchell
ISBN 1 905222 45 9 PBK £7.50

Winner of Boardman Tasker Prize for
Mountain Literature

To some, climbing is all and everything
else is nothing. But it's not just hills
– it's people, characters, fun and
tragedy – and *A View from the Ridge*
gives an authentic, enthusiastic take
on this sub-culture of adventure and
friendship – all-night card games,
monumental hangovers, storytelling,
singing – and above all, free spirits.

This essential companion to the classic
Mountain Days and Bothy Nights
captures perfectly the inexplicable
desire which brings Scottish
hillwalkers back to the mist, mud and
midgies every weekend. The lively,
humorous narrative will revitalise the
drive in you to get out on the hills – or
just to curl up on the couch with this
book and a wee dram for company.

*If you buy only one mountain book
this year make it this 'view from the
ridge' and savour its rich, different and
fascinating reflections.* Kevin Borman,
HIGH MOUNTAIN MAGAZINE

On the Trail of Queen Victoria in the Highlands

Ian R Mitchell
ISBN 0 946487 79 0 PBK £7.99

What happens when you send a Marxist on the tracks of Queen Victoria in the Highlands? – You get a book somewhat more interesting than the usual run of the mill royalist biographies!

Ian R Mitchell took up the challenge of attempting to write with critical empathy on the peregrinations of Vikki Regina in the Highlands, and about her residence at Balmoral, through which a neo-feudal fairyland was created on Upper Deeside.

The expeditions, social rituals and iconography of that world are explored and exploded from within, in what Mitchell terms a Bolshevisation of Balmorality. He follows in Victoria's footsteps throughout the Cairngorms and beyond, to the further reaches of the Highlands. On this journey, a grudging respect and even affection for Vikki ('the best of the bunch') emerges.

The English Spy

Donald Smith
ISBN 1 905222 82 3 PBK £8.99

He was a spy among us, but not known as such, otherwise the mob of Edinburgh would pull him to pieces.
JOHN CLERK OF PENICUIK

Union between England and Scotland hangs in the balance. Propagandist, spy and novelist-to-be Daniel Defoe is caught up in the murky essence of eighteenth-century Edinburgh – cobblestones, courtesans and kirkyards. Expecting a godly society in the capital of Presbyterianism, Defoe engages with a beautiful Jacobite agent, and uncovers a nest of vipers.

Subtly crafted... and a rattling good yarn. Stewart Conn

Delves into the City of Literature, and comes out dark side up. Marc Lambert

Excellent... a brisk narrative and a vivid sense of time and place. THE HERALD

Luath Press Limited

committed to publishing well written books worth reading

LUATH PRESS takes its name from Robert Burns, whose little collie Luath (Gael., swift or nimble) tripped up Jean Armour at a wedding and gave him the chance to speak to the woman who was to be his wife and the abiding love of his life. Burns called one of The Twa Dogs Luath after Cuchullin's hunting dog in Ossian's Fingal. Luath Press was established in 1981 in the heart of Burns country, and is now based a few steps up the road from Burns' first lodgings on Edinburgh's Royal Mile. Luath offers you distinctive writing with a hint of unexpected pleasures.
Most bookshops in the UK, the US, Canada, Australia, New Zealand and parts of Europe, either carry our books in stock or can order them for you. To order direct from us, please send a £sterling cheque, postal order, international money order or your credit card details (number, address of cardholder and expiry date) to us at the address below. Please add post and packing as follows: UK – £1.00 per delivery address; overseas surface mail – £2.50 per delivery address; overseas airmail – £3.50 for the first book to each delivery address, plus £1.00 for each additional book by airmail to the same address. If your order is a gift, we will happily enclose your card or message at no extra charge.

Luath Press Limited
543/2 Castlehill
The Royal Mile
Edinburgh EH1 2ND
Scotland
Telephone: 0131 225 4326 (24 hours)
Fax: 0131 225 4324
email: sales@luath. co.uk
Website: www. luath.co.uk